FIRST SNOW

"I'm afraid you've missed church," Dominic said.

"Did I? I'm sorry to hear it. I was hoping to go, but I was so very tired."

"So was I," he said. "I always sleep better in the country. So much quieter than town."

"Especially with the snowfall. What a delightful surprise for my first day here."

"I'm so happy you're pleased with it."

"Did you do it?" she asked with a smile.

"Of course. I'm on the best of terms with the snow elves."

"Snow elves?" Sophie almost laughed out loud.

"Absolutely. Didn't you' know they make the snow? My good girl, what sort of upbringing have you had? Never heard of the snow elves?"

"I'm sadly ignorant of meteorology. It wasn't considered a necessary study for females."

"How unfair."

"You must think me shockingly ignorant."

"It's not your fault. Shall I teach you all about them? Maybe you can learn to see them if you study very hard."

"You must think me about ten years old, your Grace."

"I? I assure you, quite the contrary . . ."

BOOKS BY CYNTHIA PRATT

THE BLACK MASK

A YULETIDE TREASURE

MISS LINDEL'S LOVE

LADY ROMA'S ROMANCE

A DUKE FOR CHRISTMAS

Published by Kensington Publishing Corporation

A DUKE FOR CHRISTMAS

CYNTHIA PRATT

ZEBRA BOOKS
KENSINGTON PUBLISHING CORP.
http://www.kensingtonbooks.com

ZEBRA BOOKS are published by

Kensington Publishing Corp.
850 Third Avenue
New York, NY 10022

All Kensington titles, imprints and distributed lines are available at special quantity discounts for bulk purchases for sales
promotion, premiums, fund-raising, educational or institutional
use.

Special book excerpts or customized printings can also be created to fit specific needs. For details, write or phone the office
of the Kensington Special Sales Manager: Kensington Publishing Corp., 850 Third Avenue, New York, NY 10022. Attn.
Special Sales Department. Phone: 1-800-221-2647.

Zebra and the Z logo Reg. U.S. Pat. & TM Off.

First Printing: October 2004
10 9 8 7 6 5 4 3 2 1

Printed in the United States of America

*Dedicated to my family
for putting up with the madness . . .
again.*

CHAPTER ONE

Seaside towns were all the same, Dominic thought, wind-worn, sun-faded, and smelly. He swung down from his weary horse, patting it absently as he sniffed hesitantly at the comingling scents of salty air, fish past its best, and the underlying tang of a coaching yard. Yet Dover, at this visit, held a certain enchantment, and not merely because it was the end of a tiring journey.

"Which way to the docks?" he asked a passing lounger.

"The docks, sir?" the man repeated, his good eye looking past Dominic at the splashed coach, the driver and the footmen drinking away the dryness in their throats. The coach had a coat of arms on the door, rather a gaudy one with its daubs of red and blue showing bravely through the dust and mud. The good eye became brighter, the manner more subservient, the air of greed pronounced.

"Yes. I'm meeting a ship which should have arrived today from Italy."

"Italy, sir? That 'ud be the *Aten de Mui*, Marseilles and Palermo. I'll show you to 'er meself."

Recognizing the name as the *Attendez Moi* and the names of the ports as vaguely resembling those visited by the ship he'd come to meet, Dominic agreed and followed the man out of the coaching yard, throwing a word to Fissing to see to their accommodations. The valet, nearly as tall as Dominic but half his weight, bowed with that degree of affront that told his master his words were wasted. Of course Fissing would arrange all to fit the most exacting taste. It was Fissing's misfortune that his master's taste was not at all meticulous. Dominic knew he disappointed his servant, but Fissing was an inheritance and would never consider serving any but the Duke of Saltaire.

The breeze that hit them as they came out of the sheltered yard made the lounger shiver and wrap his arms about himself. He cast a bleary eye toward the dim sun. "It'll be settling in for snow ere long," he said.

"No doubt, it being nearly December," Dominic agreed civilly, striding along with his greatcoat open.

"Ain't you cold, sir?" the lounger asked suddenly, as if taken by a sudden irresistible curiosity.

"No. Is it far to the docks?"

"Just down 'ere."

Dover bustled even on a short winter's day. Men in uniforms either naval or merchant strode along in pairs like nuns, hands clasped loosely behind their backs. Everyone else hurried. Fishmongers pushed among the crowd, the crates on their shoulders leaving redolent ribbons of fishy smells behind them.

Prosperous-looking men rushed about, stopping to greet each other and then hurrying away. What few women he could see hastened along, just as intent on reaching their goals as the men. Boys darted between, through, and sometimes over obstacles, whether human, animal, or inanimate. The alehouses seemed to be doing a roaring trade, Dominic noticed, though even there men seemed to slug down their beer and demand their refills with great rapidity. The only creatures that didn't seem infected by this mania for hustle were the huge draft horses patiently waiting for someone to unload their carts of crates and barrels.

"Oh, this ain't nothing, sir," the lounger said when Dominic asked if it was market day. "Should have seen it in the War. Couldn't hardly move for sailors and their doxies. Speakin' of which, sir, seeing as you be new in town . . ."

"Is there another way to return to my inn? A less crowded way?"

"Not so straight a course, but if you take your bearings wit' care . . . never tell me a big cove like yourself's scared of a crowd."

"I shall have a lady with me and I can't ask her to charge a line of fishmongers."

"A lady? Be it your wife?"

"No. Not my wife."

The basins and piers of the harbor were so filled with shipping that Dominic could hardly believe there had ever been more, even in wartime. The lounger took in a deep lungful of the salty air. Between coughs, he gave Dominic to understand that it was a good time to make port.

The strong breeze set all the masts to bowing and nodding as if in some dance, with the gulls overhead calling the steps. Dominic put a hand up to tug his low-crowned hat more securely onto his head. "Lead on, MacDuff," he said.

"My name's Boltoff."

"Even better. Which ship is the *Attendez Moi*?"

"Out there," Boltoff said, pointing to a black dot on the sparkling waves. "She's not come in yet. Doctors still aboard."

"Doctors?"

"Never worry, cully. They're just checking her over. Can't bring infeckuous diseases into ol' Blighty."

"I see. How long will they be?"

"Can't rightly say. Usually takes an hour or so, depending on which medico you draw. Come on. I'll show you a snug harbor where you can wait."

The thought of entering one of those raucous public houses did not appeal. "Do you know where she'll berth?"

"Not a hundred miles from where you're standin', cully. Brung you to the very spot."

Dominic fished in the pocket of his greatcoat, pulling out half a crown. "Will you come back when the ship comes in and show me the quieter way back to the coaching house?" he asked, handing it over.

"That I will. And you needn't worry that I'll drink it away. I'm not a drinking man, me."

Glancing around, Dominic saw an upended cask and sat down upon it. He was aware that Boltoff stood some distance away, watching him. His own attention was fixed upon that distant dot which he hoped was indeed the *Attendez Moi*, fresh from Marseilles and Palermo. He wished he'd had the foresight to bring a telescope, though at this distance, while it might have brought the ship into nearer view, it would not have shown him any details of the rigging, the crew, or the passengers.

Was she aboard? Or had some mishap delayed her in Marseilles? Was she, even now, looking toward this spot where she would soon step foot once more upon her native land? Three years and more since she'd left England, three years that had brought many changes in her life and in his.

Dominic sighed heavily. No doubt his imagination was running off with him again. In all probability, Sophie Banner was down below, organizing her belongings before disembarkation. Even when he'd first seen her, radiant with a bride's joy, there'd been some-

thing about her that spoke of determination and adept-
ness. They'd been introduced but had hardly spoken
until he came upon her the night before her wedding.

She'd been arranging the table placement for dinner.
He'd leaned against the door frame, watching her with
pleasure, her movements so neat and deft that she never
knocked into a wineglass or disturbed a flower's petal.
Even when he'd suddenly spoken aloud his complimen-
tary thoughts, she'd not jumped or allowed her hand to
shake. She'd only looked up at him and smiled.

"Thank you. You're Kenton's dearest friend, aren't
you?"

"Yes, I suppose I could claim that distinction."

"And are you pleased he has married my sister?"

"Very pleased. The Lindel family seems to be a very
nice one to join. Are there any other Lindels?"

"Only my mother, sir. As she is a widow, she may
welcome a new suitor." She didn't wait for him to answer. "Come and help me with this puzzle."

"What puzzle?"

"This arrangement of the place cards. We are to dine
with the women on one side of the table and the gentlemen on the other, and organizing it is driving me to
distraction." A tendril of pale gold hair had slipped from
the high knot to curve along her cheek. She puffed at it,
blowing it aside.

"I would have thought it an easier task than the other.
At least you needn't worry about putting married cou-
ples together."

"Tell me what those first two read, will you?" she
asked, pointing across the table.

Obediently, Dominic read off the names of two Miss
Pebbletons. "Ondrea and Aurilla . . . is that right?"

"Dreadful names, aren't they? I would not doubt that

is why they are both so ill-tempered. Imagine going through life as an Ondrea."

"No worse than my own name. It's Dominic."

"Oh, but I like that."

"You wouldn't if you were a boy. I cannot tell you—certainly I cannot tell *you*—all that they called me at school."

A faint deepening appeared in the tender rose of her cheeks as she laughed. "No, you shouldn't tell me. Nor should I confess that I can readily imagine what a nasty boy's imagination might do to your name. At any rate, move Miss Aurilla down about four places. Who would that put her beside?"

He read off two names and she nodded.

"Quite unexceptional. She'll find it hard to quarrel with either of them. Mrs. Dryer talks only about her sons and Mrs. Pensonby is hard of hearing. Now, who have we put beside Miss Pebbleton?"

"Miss Norbury."

"Oh dear. Miss Pebbleton dislikes her even more than she dislikes her sister."

"Shall I put Mrs. Dryer there?"

"I suppose you'd better. Move Miss Norbury back. Now what shall I do with these two men? They've been arguing for six months over a boundary dispute and I won't have settlements and messuages in the middle of my last dinner on this earth as an unencumbered female."

"You see marriage as an encumbrance?" Dominic asked, intrigued.

"Every human tie burdens one to a greater or lesser extent. If you are a conscientious person, at any rate."

"I suppose one feels an obligation not to injure people one is fond of," Dominic agreed.

"Well, I try not to. Of course, it can be complicated

when someone is fond of you and you cannot return that feeling with the same fervor."

"Sometimes hurting someone is the only way to be kind."

"You speak as if you have someone specific in mind. It must be difficult to be in your position, Your Grace."

As usual, Dominic felt embarrassed by his grand title. "Please call me Dominic, as your brother-in-law does. I can't get used to being called 'Your Grace.'"

"You haven't had the title long, from what Kenton tells me."

"The ink on the papers is scarcely dry."

"I shall call you Dominic tonight but tomorrow, when I am Mrs. Banner, it wouldn't be proper to do it any more. My husband might not like it."

"He's a poet, isn't he?"

"Yes. A very great poet."

There was such a light of love in her face that Dominic could scarcely bear to look at her without feeling intense embarrassment. She was so rapturously beautiful that she reminded him of spring flowers and the glow of summer sunsets, everything that was fresh and good in this world. And for whom did all these lights and wonders appear? A weedy poet who seemed in their one conversation to take her adoration as being no less than what was due to someone so marvelously gifted as himself.

Late that same evening, when poet and guests had taken themselves off to bed, Dominic had paced the brick garden path. Kenton was a notable amateur botanist whose blooms were the envy of rose fanciers the world over. Their heavy scent seemed stronger and sharper under the moon than in the heat of the day. He could never after smell roses without the pointed shame of that evening returning to him as if it had just occurred.

Dominic had heard her step and known it for hers before he turned. She seemed surprised to see him, and he realized that the dark of his evening attire had let him blend into the shadows of the hedge-lined walk. "Is that you, Dominic?" she asked, her low voice acting on him more powerfully than the perfumed air. "It's so late I didn't think anyone else would be awake."

"What are you doing here?" he asked, hardly recognizing his own voice.

"I couldn't sleep. I didn't want to waste this last evening."

"Your last unencumbered evening."

"That's right." She came to stand beside him. He saw that her hair, silvered by the inconstant light, flowed freely over her shoulders. The color of her pink evening dress had faded into white, and her eyes were deep and dark as she looked up at him with friendly concern. "Are you not tired either?"

"I don't know." He hardly knew what he was saying. Dominic was only surprised he hadn't been struck dumb entirely. Men weren't supposed to be susceptible to moonlight and roses. But some magic was working on him, filling him with temptation, as if some small voice were whispering urgent persuasions in his ear.

Feeling as if his hand didn't belong to him, he raised it and placed it on her shoulder. She startled, but didn't move away. The silk of her hair was cool beneath the heel of his hand, while the heat of her skin seemed to melt his fingertips. "I . . . "

"Yes?"

Dominic kissed her, surprising himself more, possibly, than he surprised her. He felt that they fit together as though they'd been carved from the same block and had at last found each other. Though not without experience with women, Dominic had never known a kiss to feel so right. He wished the moment might be prolonged infinitely, but she stirred as though she wanted to speak. Wanting to hear her voice again, prepared to overcome all her objections, he raised his head.

"My goodness gracious me." She stood back from him, a little unsteadily. Dominic hadn't realized he'd dragged her onto her toes until she stepped down.

"Sophie," he said, tasting her name for the first time. "Sophie, you mustn't marry that man. That posturing poet."

"Broderick?"

"Broderick. What can he offer you? If he makes ten pounds a year by his pen, I'd be amazed. I've been a scribbler half my life and I know."

"Yes, Ken said you'd been a writer. Grub Street?"

"That's right. I was a Grub Street hack, selling my soul for a penny a line. I don't have to do that now. I can offer you everything, a fortune, a title if you care for that, and . . . and my heart."

"Your heart?" The lightness vanished from her tone. "Oh, dear. I didn't imagine for a moment . . ." Even by moonlight, Dominic could see embarrassment in her eyes. "You see, I was talking to some of the ladies . . . women do chatter so . . . and they one and all seemed to regret that they had not taken more advantage of their opportunities when younger. Flirting and such, if you see what I mean."

"No, I'm sorry." Dominic didn't think this sounded as if Sophie were working up to an acceptance. Perhaps she hadn't realized he'd just proposed?

"Well, most of them are married, you see, and had only one man in their lives. And they were saying how they wished they'd not been so missish when men tried to kiss them when they were younger, not realizing how few men would wish to when they were married and settled. So when you looked as if you wanted to kiss me . . ." She peeped at him shyly. "I think that third glass of champagne might have been too much. I do apologize, Your Grace."

"Wait," Dominic said, reaching out as if to mesmerize her into staying. "I don't expect you to feel the same way I do, but you can't marry that dreary little tick."

"He's not really the way you saw him tonight," she said. "He's shy and his politics are something radical. He doesn't know how to behave around dukes and lords and such, so he's sometimes a little rude."

"He wasn't rude in the least. He toadied me to the top of his bent."

This seemed to strike a spark of anger in her. "I'm sure you must be mistaken," she said, her chin rising proudly. "Broderick despises all the nobility. It's a point of honor with him to treat all men as equals."

"Then he must toadeat everyone he meets. I've only been a duke a short time, but I've already learned how to spot a sycophant at a hundred yards. Your precious Broderick is the type who truckles by pretending to see no difference between men, yet all the while his eyes are toting up the cost of your boots and your signet ring. I expect him to ask me at the wedding breakfast to subscribe to an edition of his poems."

"Good night, Your Grace."

Dominic felt the humble desire of every lover to grovel unashamedly before the beloved object's frown. "No, wait. I didn't mean it. I'm sure your poet's a fine fellow, once you get to know him. But he's all wrong for you. You . . . you're wonderful."

She paused, half turned away yet listening, and Dominic hurried on. "You deserve so much more than he can give you. And I don't mean only the material goods of life, houses, jewels, fine clothes. You deserve someone who'll adore you lifelong. That poet can't see you for thinking about his wonderful self. I'd put you first and foremost. My every thought would be to please you."

"How much champagne did *you* have?" she asked, a smile in her voice. Then she looked at him. "I'm sorry. You are serious."

"Very serious. Don't you believe in love at first sight?"

"I . . . I'm not sure." Sophie glanced toward the house. "It's quite impossible."

Dominic stepped up to stand beside her. "Why?" he whispered, his breath moving the tendrils beside her ear. "Because there's a houseful of people who expect to see you married in the morning?"

She put her small hand on his shoulder and looked into his eyes. "No. Because Broderick needs me."

Perhaps his expression reflected his scorn, for she hastened to bolster her argument. "He does, indeed he does. He's so foolish about things like bills and eating regularly and keeping his clothes mended. He needs me to look after him and I . . . I need someone to look after."

"But I . . ." Dominic said, framing frantic words to protest that he needed her too.

"You have everything to offer a woman, Your Grace. You have the whole world at your feet, and I don't know how to tell you how moved I am that you have said such things to me." She touched her cheek with the fingertips of her other hand, as if soothing away a blush that the moonlight hid from him. "But I only want my poet and he only wants me. So I thank you and I bid you good night."

Then she was gone and Dom's hands reached out to capture the night air and the remembrance of a few stolen moments. He watched her marry his rival the next morning and did not stay for the wedding breakfast. The only moment he could think of afterward without wanting to hide under a rock was when she kissed him. The fact that she'd even considered the embraces of another man told him that Broderick Banner was the wrong man for her, whether she'd admit it or not.

Of course, he hadn't wasted much time repining. After a while, he'd taken to marveling at his own folly. What would he have done if she'd agreed to go with him to Gretna? Dominic told himself he'd had a narrow escape and threw himself into the follies and fun available to a young, wealthy, and titled gentleman. Yet at least once a month, Sophie Lindel Banner would appear in his dreams, always warm and smiling, inviting him to follow her into the realms of sleep, where anything might happen but never quite did.

His dreams were in his thoughts now as he waited for the *Attendez Moi* to make port. It had been slightly more than three years since that night in the garden at Finchley Place. The girl who had married the next day wouldn't be on that ship. Too much had happened. He wasn't that impulsive anymore.

Dominic reminded himself that he was here only because Kenton had requested this service of him. So far as his behavior went, he was meeting the sister-in-law of his oldest friend in order to give her his protection on the journey to her home. That evening of moonlit madness had happened to two other people a world away. He wouldn't mention it, wouldn't even think about it. The man who had offered Sophie Lindel his heart had nothing to do with him. Furthermore, there wasn't even a Sophie Lindel anymore. Only Sophie Banner, whom he had yet to meet.

It was with this resolution in mind that he stood on the

dock an hour later, looking up at the tumble-home sides of a ship. The *Attendez Moi* was far from sizable, her paint sun-faded and chipped, the sails—now sagging down—dun-colored, and the crew as unkempt as rescued castaways.

A woman stood by the railing, her boat cloak falling straight from her shoulders to the deck. Pink flooded her cheeks as she put up a hand to capture the floating strands of golden hair that had fallen from the knot on the back of her head. Her gaze swept over the docks, not as if she were looking for anything in particular but as though she were simply absorbing everything she could see.

Even if he hadn't recognized her, Dom's gaze would have been irresistibly drawn to her. Her face bore an expression of breathless anticipation, half joy, half dread. Dominic wondered whether he himself bore a similar expression. She obviously hadn't seen him. He wished with sudden violence that he hadn't come to collect her, no matter how beholden he might be to Kenton and his wife.

As he watched, trying to decide whether to dodge behind some barrels or just stand out in clear sight, she turned away with a start. A man appeared to stand beside her at the railing. Dominic didn't like the look of him at all. He had a pleasant, open face with wide apart eyes that gave him an innocent air at odds with his extremely high forehead. They didn't stand there for long. The man said something and Sophie nodded with a smile, stepping away from Dom's sight.

It seemed to take forever until the crew slid out the gangplank. Dominic occupied himself by pacing. Growing warm, he'd taken off his coat, throwing it over a barrel. He didn't notice the cold, though everyone who hurried past was muffled up to the eyes against the sharp breeze blowing off the sea.

The grinding fall of the gangplank brought him instantly to the edge of the dock. She wasn't the first person off the boat. The *Attendez Moi* didn't carry very many passengers and those who did disembark were not notable for their *ton,* being mostly shabby-genteel tourists and clerks about their business. A large family took considerable time to travel from the top of the gangplank to the bottom, the mother being troubled over some missing parcels.

"Is that the lovebirds, Mary? No? Who has the lovebirds? Did you remember to collect the spoons, Arthur? I don't want to leave the spoons. Oh, have you the lovebirds, William? I thought Mary had them. Well, then, who has Baby? Someone must go back for Baby. And the French poppet. Eva will be dreadfully upset if we forget . . . oh, you have Baby, Arthur? Then who has the spoons? And who has the poppet?"

The whole party stopped in the middle of the gangplank, which bowed under their combined weight, while a child ran back to look for whatever miscellany they'd forgotten. Dominic met the eyes of the father of this hapless band in a look of male sympathy. The father ushered the rest of his family down to the ground with a murmured, "Mustn't impede the others, my dear," placing a guiding hand under his wife's elbow.

No sooner had she reached solid ground than she tottered and clutched her husband's supporting arm. "Oh, mercy, how the ground heaves!"

With open hand, Dominic indicated his coat-draped barrel. Once seated, the woman closed her eyes, her hand pressed to her bosom. "Better," she breathed.

"Thank you, sir," the father said. Their children ranged in age from an infant in a basket to a young man blushing furiously for his parents' imposition on a stranger.

"Are you unwell, Mrs. Gibbs?" A swirl of a boat cloak passed him. Dominic turned to find Sophie on one knee beside the barrel.

"She has yet to regain her land legs, Mrs. Banner," Mr. Gibbs said.

"Oh, yes. My maids are in the same condition. I myself feel more than a trifle off balance."

"Maids?" Dominic asked, looking around. This wasn't at all how he'd imagined their meeting. He'd expected at least an acknowledgment of his presence and had hardly anticipated so many witnesses. Two young women, both blondes, stood beside a small heap of hand luggage, leaning on one another and looking about them with wide eyes.

Sophie looked over her shoulder and smiled. "Hello, Dominic, it's good to see you. Have you met the Gibbs family?"

"Were you waiting for our dear Mrs. Banner?" This new interest straightened Mrs. Gibbs's sagging spine. Under her raised eyebrows, she showed a pair of astonishingly sharp eyes. They were kindly but penetrating, oddly so for such a preoccupied woman. She studied Dominic with profound attention.

"I've come to take her home," he said, trying to not feel like a schoolboy caught stealing a pie. "Her mother and sister are waiting for her at home."

"Indeed?" she said suspiciously. Dominic began to wish he'd dressed more conservatively. Though his clothes were of the highest quality, with no aspirations toward dandyism, he did not dress like a parson or a solicitor or some other male with whom one might trust a widow. He dressed for the position he held in a nice taste which was his own and his tailor's. It was evident by the look in Mrs. Gibbs's eye that not even a long white beard would have allayed her suspicions of his being a vile seducer.

"They could not come," Sophie said clearly. "As I told you, ma'am, my sister is expecting her first child very soon and should not travel so far."

"Very wise," Mrs. Gibbs said. "I have known the gravest injury to both mother and child through such imprudence. My cousin Eudora, for instance . . ."

The conversation threatened to become obstetrical when Sophie stood up too quickly, swayed a little, and held out a faltering hand to Dominic. "Oh, dear. How long do sea legs last?"

"Not long," he said, taking her hand in his, finding it stronger and harder than he remembered. There was muscle there that hadn't come from embroidery. Her face, too, had changed. The soft contours of youth had passed, leaving a finely sculpted jaw and more evident cheekbones. Her eyes met his with steady friendliness and no trace of embarrassment. They might never have kissed under the full moon.

CHAPTER TWO

Sophie hadn't realized how much bloom she had lost until she saw Dominic Swift again. She had expected to see him sometime, of course. That would be inevitable. But she'd never imagined that it would be after a long sea journey, her hair askew, her clothes wrinkled, her skin pale and shiny, an incipient spot she could feel growing beside her nose. *When one meets an old admirer, one wishes still to be admirable,* she thought. Not that any of it really mattered; she had traveled a long way in every sense of the word from the garden at Finchley when he'd so charmingly expressed his admiration.

"The journey?" she repeated. "It was not difficult once we departed Italy. The boat left early, but then it came back, so we sailed on it after all."

"I see," he said. His voice had deepened and slowed over the intervening period. "Who are these people?"

"The Gibbses? They've been traveling through Italy for the children's health."

"No, not them. Them." He waggled a finger subtly at Angelina and Lucia, standing by the luggage at the foot of the gangplank.

"They are my landlady's daughters," Sophie said. "I couldn't afford to pay the last three months' rent, you see, so I agreed to bring them to England." She refused to be embarrassed or coy about her financial difficulties. They were, after all, the chief reason for her return to her native country.

"As hard **up as** that?" he asked, a certain humorous respect coming into his eyes.

"Even more so. I had to sell my furniture for the fares. Besides, I like them very much. I have promised to teach them how to be ladies' maids and to write them excellent references."

She stood up to go to them and felt his hand warm on her arm. "And the man?"

"Man?" Sophie followed his gaze and saw Mr. Knox talking to the girls. His Italian was not as good as hers, but both Angelina and Lucia were paying close attention, not giggling as they usually did when any non-Italian tried to speak to them.

"Oh, that's Clarence Knox. He was a friend of my husband's. He's a poet, too."

Mr. Knox looked up and caught sight of her. He smiled at her in the way that she'd come half-consciously to dread. It held too much warmth, too much hope. One she could not return, and the other she could not bring herself to dash. Now they had come home, this friendship she had inherited would fade without the necessity of hurting his feelings. It could never ripen into anything else. Mr. Knox resembled Broderick too much in tone of mind to attract her. Besides, her tastes had never run to men shorter than herself with hair carefully brushed to conceal its thinning. Even that wouldn't have prevented her if she'd found almost childlike round blue eyes and snub noses appealing.

Dominic followed her across the dock, his footsteps firm and slow. She'd forgotten how tall he was. "Your

Grace, may I present Mr. Clarence Knox? Mr. Knox, this is the Duke of Saltaire."

Mr. Knox actually took a step back, as anyone might when suddenly confronted with an inoffensive young man who turned out to have a title and a fortune reputed to be majestic in scope. Dominic hardly seemed to notice the man's reaction. Perhaps he was used to it by now.

They shook hands in that very cool English style. Sophie compared it to the sometimes overwhelming enthusiasm of the Italian male and knew she had truly come home.

"Could you tell them where to send the luggage?" she asked Dominic, indicating the several crew members bringing down trunks on their shoulders. Most were dumped in front of the Gibbses.

"Certainly," he said, stepping away.

"I had no notion that you were acquainted with anyone of such high degree," Mr. Knox said in her ear. "Is that the famous Duke of Saltaire?"

"Famous? I don't know if I would describe him so."

"Come now, you must know the story. How he was a poverty-stricken nobody until careful investigation uncovered the truth. I believe Armstrong Blevely was writing an epic on the subject."

"Armstrong wrote many an epic—in his head," Sophie said tartly. "Never a one on paper that I ever heard tell of. The last I heard, he'd taken a position in his uncle's relish manufactory." Her late husband had poured scorn on the fallen poet for his choosing Gentlemen's Pickle over the divine fire, but Sophie herself only wished that there'd been a going concern connected with the name of Banner, even if it had been connected with marmalade or horseshoe nails.

"Alas, poor Blevely," Mr. Knox said, shaking his head.

"Still, it's a tale worthy of an epic. I heard tell he was working in a blacksmith's when they told him he was the heir to a dukedom."

"No. He was a writer."

"A writer?"

"Grub Street, I believe. But we've never actually discussed the matter." Not, at least, in any circumstances that she'd care to share.

"What a fate to befall one," Mr. Knox said, half to himself. "So much wealth and fine position and all through a mere accident of fate." He smiled at her, returning to the present. "Ah, well, no such fairies attended my christening," he said ruefully. "My father was a simple justice of the peace whose family line was as clear as a black line upon white paper. Not the slightest chance that some surprising rich relations will suddenly point to me and say, 'Thou art the man to inherit my riches.' More's the pity. I shall have to win my fortune by other means."

"Your pen, perhaps?"

His eyes suddenly moist, Mr. Knox reached out to grasp her hands. "Poor Broderick was taken from us too soon," he said earnestly. "I know, had he lived longer, we all would have been the better for it. Not just you, his loving wife, and I, his dearest friend, but the world will suffer from the loss of his talents, whether it knows it or not."

"Yes," she said, moved more for his sake than for her own. "I shall do what I can to bring his work to the world."

"Then you mean to proceed with publication?"

"If I can. I owe it to his memory."

He raised her hands to his chest and pressed them there. "If I can be of any assistance in this great work, I pray . . . I beg . . . you will call upon me. Though you kept Broderick's heart, I feel I had some insight into the workings of his mind. I would gladly give all my time to your aid."

With an effort, she freed her captive hands. "You're too kind, Mr. Knox. I have your address in town. If I need your help, be assured I shall call for it."

Sophie became aware that Dominic waited for her. With a bright smile that belied her true feelings, she said good-bye to Mr. Knox. Picking up one of her valises, she motioned to the two Italian girls to follow her. "*Andiamo, mia ragazzi*. Follow the gentleman."

Dominic seemed to be scanning the faces of the dockside idlers. "Ah, there he is," he said. "And he's brought a barrow for your baggage."

"Your servant?" she asked, eyeing the ragtag figure approaching.

"No, but I'm considering attaching him to my service. He's an unusual character. I'd best not, though. He'd give my valet an apoplexy."

Strange to walk arm-in-arm with anyone but Broderick. Dominic Swift was much taller than her late husband, and Sophie was surprised to find how comforting it was to press through a crowd with him. His care to guard her from the carelessness of passing strangers was equaled by his ability to do so. No one had ever stepped aside for Broderick, no matter how he swaggered. But roads seemed to open when Dominic came near and it couldn't be that everyone knew who he was. He wasn't *that* famous.

She kept her eyes upon the two girls, smiling at them reassuringly whenever they looked back. Angelina was rolling her eyes from side to side like a frightened horse, amazed and frightened by strange sights, sounds, and smells. Lucia also looked around her, but, as had been true from the start of their acquaintance, it was with lively curiosity and the most intense desire to acquire knowledge. Before them, as if leading a procession, came the beached sailor, pushing the barrow and keeping up a constant commentary as if he'd appointed himself guide and preceptor to the two foreigners, little though they might understand.

It seemed a long way to the inn. She had cause to be glad of Dom's arm. "I am not accustomed to walking more than the length of the deck," she panted at the top of a hill. "I had no notion I was so out of condition."

"Do you still feel the motion of the boat?"

"Not so much, though I should be glad to sit down. And, oh, a cup of tea. Real tea. I've been dreaming of it every night."

"Don't they have tea in Italy?"

She peeped up at him suspiciously. Was he laughing at her? His face remained grave but there was a smile in his voice.

"Yes, they do. But it's rather expensive and somehow never tastes right. I think it's the water in Rome."

His smile broke through his reserve. "I think the Golden Hind will run to a cup of tea. Perhaps even an entire pot."

"Then let's hurry." Having caught her breath, she tried to pull him along. She might as well have tried to pull the *Attendez Moi,* though he consented to move at last with a resigned smile upon his face.

When she reached her bedchamber, the landlady was there, stripping the sheets off the bed. "Oh, I beg your pardon," Sophie said, hesitating on the threshold.

"You are Mrs. Banner? That valet told me to change your linen. As if sheets in my house are ever damp!"

She stood with her hands on her thin hips, her woolen overskirt kilted up to show a flowered flannel petticoat underneath. Her white cap was shoved back on her graying hair and she bore harassed lines on her fore-head.

"I'm sorry for the extra trouble," Sophie said. "What valet is this?"

"A lanky pin-shanks by the name of Fissing. He's poked his long nose into my kitchens, dug in my cellars, and sneered at my sheets. I'll pull his long nose if I see it again, so help me."

"He's the Duke's man?"

"Aye, he is. To hear him speak, you'd think this house had never entertained any titled folk before. Why, the Earl of Kinton himself was pleased to praise my shortbread. And Lady Moira O'Connell told me that if I ever was wishful to stop running this inn, she'd take me on as housekeeper without a second thought. And at a very good stipend too, for all it'd mean living in Ireland."

Though tired and desiring nothing more than a few minutes of quiet before the fire in a room that did not swoop with wave and wind, Sophie set herself to calming the landlady's ruffled feathers. She stepped forward to catch the upper edge of the fresh sheet to pull it straight. "Mmm," she hummed, breathing in. "Is that lavender I smell? Such a pleasant change from the ship's bilges."

"So I should think indeed. Never will I lay a sheet away without sprigs of dried herbs between. Keeps off the moth and keeps the cupboard sweet. Now, never you mind, mis-sus . . ."

"It's no trouble," Sophie said brightly, reaching for a pillowcase. "Many hands make light work, you know, Mrs—?"

"Cricklewood, ma'am. Mrs. Thomas Cricklewood. He's been gone to his reward these five years come Michaelmas."

"I see. Do you find it difficult to carry on here without him?"

Mrs. Cricklewood started to answer and then hesitated. A distant expression came into her eyes, as if she'd never considered the question before. Then she nodded. "There was so much to be done, and nothing to do but to see it through."

"So true," Sophie said. "The first three months are a blur to me now. Then to find a way to come home and all that that entailed with no more help than I could find from the consulate in Rome. They were kind, but there was so much to do on my own."

"You're too young to be a widow," Mrs. Cricklewood said flatly.

"I feel that, too. But here I am, nonetheless."

Mrs. Cricklewood pursed her lips and gave a last emphatic thump to the pillow. "I'll bring you some hot water and a pot of tea. Just home from foreign parts, I reckon tea's the first thing you'll care to take aboard."

"Oh, yes, please. And the two young ladies that were with me . . . where are they? They speak no English."

"They'll be one flight up, Mrs. Banner, though what you want with a pair of handless foreigners when there are good English girls going wanting . . ."

"That's a long story, but they have been good to me. I must see they are comfortable."

"Well, we all know our own business best. I'll be about your tea, if that Fissing will let me near my own kettle."

After sharing a narrow cabin for ten days with both the Ferrara sisters, being alone was the greatest possible luxury. Neither girl was a difficult companion when not seasick, though Lucia's sulky beauty attracted too much attention from the sailors. But the constant presence of other people had rubbed Sophie's soul raw. She had grown used to solitude in the last year and had treasured it.

Laying aside her bonnet and cloak, she caught sight of herself in the pier glass beside the washstand. Thanks to the cold, she'd been unable to see what the women of England were wearing under their warm outerwear. The last *Ladies' Magazine* she'd seen was eighteen months old, and even had she liked the styles, she could not have afforded a new dress.

She hardly believed herself to be in the mode, even if it might have swung back to the fashions of three years before. This dark wool day dress had been part of her bride clothes, now dyed for mourning with indifferent success. In some lights, it looked the color of the bladderwrack that floated on the sea, in others an odd bronze-green. Her mother was as clever a needlewoman as lived and had much store of fabric laid by. Surely once home, she'd find new things to wear. There was no point in taking in the waist of this dress anymore, even if it did fit her little better than her boat cloak. Food at home would be plentiful, more than enough to help her regain her former contours. She did look gaunt, her cheeks all fallen in. No one would take her for thirty, let alone a few months shy of twenty-one.

Stepping closer, she looked into her own eyes. The frankness and confidence that had once shown so bravely there were gone forever. Now she looked at the world as one who would wince if only her will would permit such a show of weakness. She could eat her fill, pinch her cheeks to make them pink, and do her hair in ringlets and ribbons, but what could she do about her eyes? *A fringe*, she thought, *or a veil*.

At a tap on the door, she called, "Come in," and, as if these were magic words, a parade of wonders entered. A maid with a silver tray loaded with translucent porcelain cups and a pot with fascinating curls of steam emerging from the spout preceded a stoutly calved youth pushing in a slipper tub. Two pert girls with brass cans of water, the cooler air condensing on the sides to send drips of water falling to the floor, were followed by a superior sort of servant in a black suit of clothes. He was very tall and thin, with a nose that could have given Wellington's two lengths and still romp home. Sophie had no difficulty identifying him, but it took considerable command to keep from laughing, for she could well imagine Mrs. Cricklewood having little patience with such an exquisite personage.

"You must be Fissing," she said. "I must thank you for all your care of me."

"His Grace's orders, ma'am," he answered with a bow correct to the millimeter for both a widow and a friend of his master's. "He asks if you would deign to dine with him this evening."

"I'd be more than happy," she said, wondering if his respectful bow factored into account her evident poverty. In this she did him an injustice, as she realized a moment later. It was his own consequence he honored, not hers. He directed the tub to be set thus, the tea tray so, and the attendant maidens could not pour the bath water until he tested it with a thermometer he withdrew from his pocket. His gracious nod of permission would have looked well coming from a bishop.

"I have taken the liberty, ma'am, of opening your bags. If it pleases you, I should like to take an iron to several of your gowns so that you may choose one for this evening."

"Thank you, Fissing. There's not much to choose from, I'm afraid."

"Black must always be proper," he said, as though

reading it off one of the tablets handed down to Moses at Mount Sinai.

"Yes, of course."

Several more journeys with cans of hot water saw the tub ready for use. Fissing had even produced a bar of scented soap. Sophie found herself wondering if Dominic used it.

Alone again, Sophie was torn between the tea she longed for and the sight of so much fresh water to be devoted to washing away the stains of travel. There'd been no water for washing on the ship, only for sponging off the more obvious marks and washing one's hands. And in Italy, in order to bathe, she herself had to carry the water from the kitchen stove up four flights of stairs, for she'd never been able to bring herself to bathe in the landlady's kitchen as Broderick did. The water was never more than lukewarm after that climb.

She decided not to ruin the tea with hurrying. Pausing to pop on the cozy, she hastily undid laces and buttons in order to slip cautiously if blissfully into the tub. True, it only came up to her hips but it felt like the waters of paradise. Soon, however, she realized that, though the water was warm and relaxing, she could not release the tension that had been holding her together since months before Broderick's death. Her bath, therefore, was brief.

"I'll be hanged before I ever leave England again," she said, sinking down before the fire to let her hair dry and pouring out at last the fragrant tea. Her first sip made her sigh with delight. Yet her worries did not leave her. Even in sleep lately, she'd been plagued by her troubles. Maybe when she saw her home again, all this tension would finally leave her. She wondered if she would fall down like a puppet when its strings are cut.

Driven by her sense of responsibility, Sophie went up-

stairs after dressing to see if the Ferrara sisters had all they
needed. At her gentle rap, Angelina came out, her finger
raised to her full lips. "*Prego, Signora,*" she said, adding
that she had just that moment seen Lucia fall asleep and
that she herself intended to rest as well.

"Shall I have dinner sent up to you?" she said carefully.

Angelina's pretty face bore a look of disgust. She spoke
rapidly, too fast and too idiomatically for Sophie to follow. Her Italian had its limits, bounded by the classics on
one side but coming to a sharp stop when it reached the
street. She gathered, however, that the sisters' interiors
were still too disturbed by the emotions attendant on
reaching land to find food other than nauseating, even if
it had been something they recognized.

Her next meal held considerable interest for Sophie.
Even if her insides had been more seriously disarranged
by travel than they were, she still would have been eager
to taste her native foodstuffs again. Her last beefsteak
had been so long ago that it was no more than a distant
memory—as a wonder glimpsed once in a dream and
never forgotten.

Whether through Mrs. Cricklewood's natural talents
or the nosiness of Fissing, dinner was all Sophie could
have hoped for and more.

At the end of a gorging three-quarters of an hour, she
glanced up, rather guiltily, at Dom. He sat on the other
side of a small round table, idly turning a wineglass in his
fingers, gazing through the ruby wine. His long legs were
stretched out before him, still in their boots. He had not
dressed for dinner, and Sophie wondered if Fissing had
vouchsafed the information that she had no evening dress
of any description.

"I'm sorry," she said, after swallowing a last bite of

cream cake. "My conversation seems to have gone all to pieces in the last few years."

His kind eyes smiled at her. "You've no idea what a pleasure it is to see a young woman eat with appetite. Most of the maidens I squire at parties and dances and such seem to think eating unladylike. They peck at their food like birds or, worse, claim they are not hungry, then snatch bits from my plate. I don't like it when a particularly tasty morsel disappears just as I am about to put a fork in it."

"You attend a great many such entertainments?"

His broad shoulders moved carelessly under his beautifully cut coat. "When friends invite me, I try not to snub them. And your sister is always most happy to find me partners. Or perhaps it is the girls who need a partner, and I am never too proud to ask anyone to dance."

"My sister gives many parties?" This did not accord with her memories of Maris.

"Several each Season. I owe your sister a great debt, and if dancing with spotty or butter-toothed girls is a way to make her happy, I shall be a willing sacrifice."

"What do you owe her?"

"She saved Ken from making a rake of himself. He was headed down that path, and it would have been a woeful waste. He's one of the few truly good men I know."

"I hadn't heard this tale. I know Maris was foolish about Sir Kenton, but I hadn't known that he was so far gone in sin."

"He had a most rapacious mistress," he said, "who would have ended by ruining him, morally if not financially. Once he met your sister, he put that other woman aside—for which act all his friends were profoundly grateful."

"I'm glad as much for Ken's sake as for Maris's. Some

women do seem to have the power to overset a man's thinking." Suddenly the second cake, the overfilled jelly glinting red as rubies in the firelight, no longer looked even remotely tempting. She knew entirely too much about bewitching women and the effect they had on husbands.

CHAPTER THREE

"What time shall we be off in the morning?" Sophie asked, turning her thoughts resolutely away from her memories.

"In the morning? I thought you would wish to spend several days here, resting from your journey."

"I suppose that would be sensible," she said.

"But you'd rather be on your way with all haste?" he asked, as if he'd read her mind.

"Have I grown so transparent?" He didn't answer with words but with a sideways glance. "Yes," she admitted, "I am eager to be at home. I have missed them all so much. But if the horses need to be rested further, of course I shall have to wait."

"We came along by easy stages, and as I will be riding, perhaps we could leave in the morning, as you have so little luggage."

"Riding," she echoed dreamily. "How I have missed that."

"They have horses in Italy, as well as tea."

"Yes, very fine horses, though a little heavy across the rump. But even the swayback rubbish-cart horses were above my touch. Which recalls something to my mind . . ."

She had learned not to be missish during battles with landladies, mistresses, and the wives of English expatriates. She'd even learned how to deal with men without making play of her femininity. But this was Dominic and the subject was money.

"I cannot afford at present to pay my shot at this inn, nor indeed to pay for anything greater in cost than six shillings and sixpence, unless Mrs. Cricklewood is willing to accept Italian scrip. I hope to be able to pay you back at some future date." Sophie hoped he'd attribute her pink cheeks to the wine she'd drunk, not embarrassment.

"Actually, Ken has equipped me with enough soft to pay for everything. Whatever restitution you feel you must make is between the two of you."

"Yes, of course." She stood up as Fissing came in to clear the table. He had not permitted the inn's servant to enter beyond the threshold of the private parlor, even carving the joint himself. Now his pale eyes flicked over the table. Sophie wished now that she'd eaten that last tart. They might not appear at table again if he thought she had not liked them.

"Dinner was wonderful, Fissing. Pass my compliments to Mrs. Cricklewood, please."

"Of course, ma'am," he said, bowing without stopping his work.

Dominic brought his wine to the fire. "He approves of you," he said softly.

"Wherever did you find him?"

"He was my grandfather's man, trained by his former valet, who must have been something of a tartar. I doubt my grandfather could call his soul his own if the teacher was anything like the pupil."

"You do look terribly ill-used." The difficult moment past, Sophie felt she could joke comfortably with him.

"Oh, I am, I am. I've had to give up comfortable boots, putting my feet on the furniture, and smoking cigars. My desk is straightened, my bills receipted, my books put away—whether I'm done reading them or not."

"That is hard to bear. Men don't like to be fussed over, that much I have learned."

"Well, Fissing fusses like a mother. Or a wife."

Sophie glanced up, surprising an expression of tenderness on his face, or so she thought. The candlelight was flickering from the draught through the opened door as Fissing departed. When she looked again, there was nothing to be seen but the cool eyes and his lips with their slightly ironical twist. He turned the conversation to Italy and drew out her opinions on art, sanitation, and differences between cultures.

"At first, you know, I was rather shocked by the way they conduct so much business in the street. Many of their homes have portals in the side that they open to sell goods. And the noise—the street today was nothing compared to it. Every transaction is conducted at the top of their voices. That took some time to adjust to, but soon there I was, shouting and laughing with the rest. There was a flower seller on the corner who never failed to give me a carnation when I went by. At first, Broderick bought all my flowers from him. Then . . ." Sophie stopped, aghast at her near betrayal. "Well, even when I couldn't afford flowers, he always gave me a carnation. Sometimes rather dashed, but still smelling so sweetly."

"Then you found friends so far from home?"

"More friends than I ever could have hoped for."

"There are many English in Rome, I believe."

"More all the time. People making a tour of Europe, of course, now that it's safer. You can always tell them. They look at the buildings, not the people, and never trouble to learn a word of the language, not even enough to drive away the more importunate vendors." She laughed a little. "Listen to me, running on as though

Rome were my own private estate overrun by vulgar hordes. People should come to Rome in flocks, yes, and spend all their money there. Heaven knows the city could use it. There is much poverty there."

"I didn't mean tourists so much," Dominic said. "There are many English who make their home there now. I've met a few on their visits home. Let me see . . . do you know Lady Devere, relict of the Earl of Grassle?"

Sophie flinched. "I don't care for the term 'relict,' especially now that I am one."

"I beg your pardon." But there was a smile in his voice.

"I have met Lady Devere, but I cannot say I care for the entourage she has gathered about herself. I'm sorry if she is a friend of yours."

"I know her son better than I know her. What is the matter with her entourage?"

Sophie shook her head. "If you know her son, then I am very glad. He should know what goes on at the Villa da Pace. Her secretary claims to have a title, which I believe he stole from a poem by Byron; there are several persons of no apparent past who have taken up residence with her; and her butler is well known to be robbing her blind. She'll hear no ill of anyone, not even of the little priest she has with her, allegedly teaching her Italian and Latin."

"What's wrong with him?"

"Nothing, except that he took every opportunity to back me into a corner and whisper . . . suggestions."

"I see," Dominic said, all laughter having left his tone. "How did you meet her?"

"Through Broderick. He knew everyone, from the man who swept the streets to the cardinal in charge of the bank at the Vatican. He had a knack for making acquaintances, if not friends."

"Why not friends?"

Sophie realized she'd been rattling on without pause for quite half an hour. "You are far too easy to talk to, Dominic," she said, standing up. "I had better retire before I bore you any further."

He rose and she realized afresh how tall he was. "I shall write to Lady Devere's son, I think, and warn him that his mother has found herself among an unsavory lot."

"Please do. She's a dear, though rather a featherbrain. Tell him she's taken to wearing a turban and drinking inferior sherry, won't you?"

"Is it important he should know that?"

"I think so. It means she is running out of money, don't you see? Those people must be a great expense, even if they don't actually steal it. If I had known whom to write, I should have done so myself."

"When did you see her ladyship last?"

"She bade me come to her villa when she discovered I meant to leave Italy. She very kindly offered me a place in her home. I told her that I wanted nothing more than to return to England, and she looked so wistful that I almost asked her to come with me. I wish now that I had."

"Do you believe that I should write to Horace tonight?"

Sophie considered the question. Did Dominic think she was an alarmist, seeing danger where there was none? Broderick had laughed at her fears, saying that worry merely brought wrinkles to her fair brow. Yet his admonition had not ceased her worrying; if anything, it had brought another set of troubles to her attention.

"I should think that Lord Devere would wish to know the circumstances. If he should wish to write to me, by all means give him the address at Finchley Old Place."

After Sophie had retired, leaving a soft scent of soap behind her, Dominic rang for Fissing, asking for wine, ink, pen, and paper. The valet brought them, all but the wine from His Grace's own supply. "Thank you," Dominic said. "Do you happen to recall where Lord Devere might be found at this season?"

"According to *The Gazette,* Your Grace, the Earl has retired to his country seat, Andringham, for the holiday season."

"And Andringham is in Sussex?"

"Essex, Your Grace."

"Ah, yes. There'll be a letter to post in the morning, Fissing."

"Very good, Your Grace."

"No, I'm afraid not. I do hate to appear a rumormonger, minding everybody's business but my own, yet this must not wait until I meet Devere again. Mrs. Banner has brought me distressing news about his mother."

"Ah, yes, a most eccentric lady. She vowed to leave England if they brought Lord Liverpool in as Prime Minister. She was true to her word."

"Yes, I remember that." He dipped his pen in the inkwell and sat for a moment, collecting his thoughts.

"Will there be anything further, Your Grace?"

"Yes, indeed, Fissing. Procure a horse."

"Your Grace?"

"A horse, suitable for a lady who has not been mounted for some three years. Not too sluggish, but not restive either. A gentle mare of four or five years. Jasper Coachman should be able to help you. By morning, if you please. We will be departing no later than ten o'clock."

"Very good, Your Grace."

Dominic felt no compunction at giving such an order. He knew well that Fissing felt his full talents were never utilized by his master. By all accounts, Dominic's grandfather had been exacting, tyrannical, and bad-mannered. The very qualities that had sent Dom's father into self-imposed exile, changing his name and hiding his lineage, had apparently attached his valets to his interest with hoops of iron. Neither the original valet nor Fissing would have turned a hair if the late Duke of Saltaire had asked for a battleship, an elephant, or a holy relic of Saint Anselm. They lived by the principle that the master was the master and the man more than a man. That Fissing could do no more for the present holder of the title than shine his boots or arrange his travel meant that the greater part of his gifts went unused and underappreciated.

As Dominic suspected, in the morning, a horse exactly as specified stood outside the inn. The mare was gray, with a lighter mane and feathers on fetlocks and hocks. A fine lady's saddle rode its back, a ribbon of gold toolwork all along the edges, matched by a bridle with brasses bright as the gold.

Dominic stood so that he could gain the best view of Sophie's face when she came out of the inn. Her reaction did not disappoint him. A surprised "Oh!" came from her lips as she stopped short upon the threshold. Her bright eyes swept over the mare, taking in her points at a glance. "What a darling!" she exclaimed. "Thank you, Fissing. Wherever did you find her?"

"A simple matter," his man said, even his humility a matter of pride.

Feeling the wind go out of his sails, Dominic watched as Sophie went to the mare, holding out her hand in greeting. "What gentle eyes," she said. "What is her name?"

"Rosamund, ma'am. She belonged to a young lady of good family. They were reluctant to sell her. However, she was not being ridden enough to continue her good health."

"What happened to the young lady?"

Dominic held up his hand in warning but Fissing ignored him magnificently. "She passed away some months ago, ma'am. Most unfortunate."

"I shall ride in her memory."

"So I took the liberty of telling her parents, ma'am."

Now, at last, Sophie looked for him. "You're very thoughtful, sir. Do you aspire to be a genie, granting every wish as soon as it is spoken?"

"Fissing is the genie," Dominic said, happy to give credit where it was due so long as she looked at him with enjoyment sparkling in her eyes.

"Then you must be the sheikh whose commands he fulfills. Thank you very much," she said with a curtsy. She looked down at herself. "Now I know why my riding dress was laid out instead of my round gown."

The green cloth had seen one too many pressings with a too hot iron. Shiny patches showed in the full skirt and a rent had been inexpertly sewn up in the right sleeve. She wore a man's hat that was slightly too big for her, tied on with a spotted scarf.

Dominic made a basket with his interlaced fingers. Sophie put her knee into it and he tossed her up into the saddle. The horse stood like a carved statue while she arranged her skirts to fall becomingly. Dominic noticed that the leather of her boots was much creased about the ankles and the heels were badly worn.

Somehow this sight brought welling up a feeling of rage against the late Broderick Banner that all his foreknowledge of the man's fecklessness had not been able to stir. What right had a poet to keep his wife from riding, from dressing decently, from eating properly? He'd noticed that everything she wore was too big in the body, as if she'd lost at least a stone since they were made for her bride clothes.

While Fissing saw that the two maids were comfortably bestowed in one carriage, Dominic went to consult with his groom and coachman about their route. He had, therefore, a few minutes to gain command of himself before he returned to Sophie. After all, one couldn't let a newly minted widow guess that one's opinion of her husband hadn't improved upon his death. He believed it wrong to speak ill of the dead, but there was no stricture upon *thinking* ill of them.

"She's beautifully behaved," Sophie said, turning the mare in a circle.

"Of course. Fissing wouldn't have stood for it, otherwise."

"You shouldn't have done it. But I'm so glad you did."

He smiled at her over the back of his own bay hack, already proved over the distance. "It was a pleasure. I don't often have the opportunity to do things for other people. Things I want to do, at any rate."

She urged the horse forward and said a few words to the girls in the carriage. They looked troubled that she would not be with them, but one of them caressed the side curtains and, glancing at Dominic, said something in her own tongue. Then, with an effort that brought a frown to her smooth brow, she said, "Pretty. Such pretty."

"My word," Dominic answered. "English."

"Very good, Angelina," Sophie said. "*Va bene.*"

The coachman mounted on the box of the carriage, the boy beside him. The berlin with the luggage would be driven by Peck, the groom, with the other boy sitting there, arms folded. Fissing had his new sheets to keep him contented. Gossip was the stuff of life to him, for only by constant application could he master the thousand and one intricacies of high life that His Grace could not be troubled to remember. Dominic suspected he never would live up to Fissing's standards of dukeliness.

It took them quite half an hour to leave Dover, thanks to the traffic in the streets. "And I thought London was bad," Dominic said, waiting behind two drays that had locked rear wheels, completely blocking the intersection.

"You should see Rome at Christmas," Sophie said. "No holiday was complete without at least two carriages overturned and a fire. The glorious races at the Coliseum couldn't be nearly so exciting."

"I think you will miss that city."

"I suppose I will miss some things about it. It can be very beautiful, especially in the early morning. There's something about the way the light comes in among the buildings. One finger of it would touch my bedroom window every morning in the spring, turning all my litter into gold. Even in winter a pale thread would reach through, reminding me that spring wasn't so far away."

She seemed almost to be speaking to herself. Dominic didn't speak but gazed at her, willing her to say more. But a fight broke out between the two dray drivers, breaking her concentration. Pressing her mare forward, she stopped on the near side of the drays and, rising in the saddle, looked over. "Please, gentlemen, I want to go home and I have many miles yet to travel."

The two men, covered in dust and not a little blood, drew apart. "Beg your pardon, ma'am. Lend a hand here, Henry."

"Aye, Silas. Comin', I am."

They were five miles beyond the town when there was at last room to let the horses do more than walk.

Dominic realized he had nothing to concern himself with. Though it may have been a few years since she'd last ridden, she'd forgotten nothing of her skill. The mare and the woman seemed alike in their longing for a faster pace and a taste of freedom.

They stopped for the night at the Gorgon's Head in Bainbridge, a more select house than Mrs. Cricklewood's. Here there was little need for Fissing's talents, though he would have gone to the stake sooner than admit it. He contented his pride by accepting even the extraordinary services with an air that said the valet wasn't the sort to denigrate those doing their best, however limited.

Though the Gorgon's Head was famous across the south of England for the splendor of its table, the landlord was not about to serve his finest dinner to the Duke of Saltaire without adding a great many extra touches. Nor would his lady guest lack any attention. The bill would be commensurate with the trouble, Dominic thought, and remembered with what pleasure he'd hosted dinners for impoverished friends when freshly come into his money.

Washed and immaculately shaved, Dominic waited in the best private parlor. A large bouquet of candles cast a dreamy, golden glow over the table, highlighting the crystal stemware and plates created from one of Mr. Wedgwood's most delightful dreams. Dried flowers gave out a faded, sweet scent over the fireplace, like ghosts of roses lingering in a place they'd loved. Dominic reminded himself that he'd ordered none of this; he was not trying to create a romantic atmosphere. Was it his fault if the management misunderstood his relationship with Sophie?

As the minutes ticked past, she did not appear. Dominic watched the candles shrink. Then, abruptly, he left the room.

"Sophie?" he asked, rapping lightly at her door. "Are you coming down to dine?"

When her voice came, it was tight. "No, I can't . . . that is, I don't believe I shall. Would you ask to have a little soup sent up to me?"

"Are you ill?"

"No, not ill." He heard her slow footsteps approach the door. Pulling open the door, she stood before him, her figure swathed in a red woolen dressing gown. Stood, however, was perhaps not quite the correct word. True, she was on her feet, but her posture seemed as hunched as an old woman's. "I think I shall drive tomorrow," she said. "There are apparently some muscles that do not like suddenly returning to horseback."

"Do you need help?"

"The Ferrara sisters have been a great comfort. Lucia is quite a talented masseur. I am hungry, though."

"I happen to know they've gone to some trouble to make a special dinner. I shall order it sent here."

"Not all of it. A glass of wine, however, would be most welcome." She smiled—or perhaps it was a spasm of pain.

"You shall have it instantly. Go, make yourself comfortable, or as comfortable as possible, and I shall have everything done at once."

"Thank you, Dominic." With a sudden gesture, she reached out to grasp his sleeve. "You are being much too kind to me. I'm not . . ." Her fingers relaxed and her hand slipped from his arm. "I'm most grateful."

"Not at all," Dominic said, wondering very much what she had begun to say. He rather fancied she'd been going to add that she wasn't used to having her comfort considered, but that might just be wishful thinking on his part. It wasn't that he wanted her husband to have been brutal to her, though he wouldn't have put it past Broderick Banner. But he wouldn't have been human if he hadn't wanted Sophie to realize just what she'd given up in choosing the poet over the duke. He was ashamed of his feelings, but they existed anyway.

He met Fissing in the dining parlor. "Mrs. Banner will eat in her room tonight. She is tired."

"Very good, Your Grace. I shall arrange matters at once."

"The very best of each dish, mind, Fissing. I only wish there were flowers at this season."

"Indeed. A table looks undressed without flowers or even a touch of Christmas greenery."

"Well, there'll be plenty of that at Finchley. Sir Kenton has asked me to stay over the Christmas season, but I think I shall return to London."

"Not Saltaire, Your Grace?"

Dominic thought of drawing up before that great, echoing house, with its forty blank windows staring down. Of white marble turning the entrance hall into a huge frozen pudding where stiff servants seemed only half thawed as they made their formal greeting to the returning master. Of the reverberating silence when he had no guests and the empty gaiety when he did bring people to share it.

"It's too late to invite friends. They all have plans by this time."

"Then shall I go ahead to Town and open the house?"

"Yes, when we return to Finchley, you and the coachman might as well proceed on to London. I won't need you at Finchley, and I can't have the horses eating Sir Kenton out of house and home. My groom can put up at the inn and watch over Phrenicos for me."

"And when may we expect Your Grace's appearance in London?"

"I'm not sure. No more than a few days. Now, if you please, Fissing, Mrs. Banner's tray?"

Fissing raised one black eyebrow in his most deprecating glance. "At once, Your Grace."

Put solidly in his place, Dominic poured another glass of wine and fell to waiting for his own dinner. He doubted very much that Sophie would ride tomorrow, but he had hopes for the day after. It could only do her good to shake off the weakness of her long constraint at sea and, he'd begun to suspect, her long entrapment in Rome.

CHAPTER FOUR

Sophie's sore muscles kept her out of the saddle for two days, for which reprieve she returned much thanks. So long as the weather remained clear, however cold, Dominic would ride and not enter the carriage. His generosity and concern for her comfort, demonstrated both by the gift of Rosamund and by his tender consideration at each inn where they stopped, were like mines laid beneath the bulwarks of her self-command. She could not control when they might explode, destroying another piece of her façade. She'd already given away far, far too much. Dominic Swift was no fool. He could put two and two together and determine a very clear answer.

Though prudence demanded a third day's travel in the carriage, the little taste she'd had of freedom and exercise made her confinement irksome. The motion of the carriage reminded her too much of the sea, with even less room for cramped muscles to stretch. Before retiring that night, she mentioned to Fissing that she would wish to ride again on the morrow.

She vowed that she would speak only of neutral subjects with Dominic: the weather, politics, and fashion. No personal matters would be permitted to intrude. If trouble arose, one could always find distractions to do with one's horse—examine an alleged loose girth or wonder if the beast had picked up a stone or, as a last resort, propose a gallop.

Judging how his eyes lit when he saw her come out in her riding costume, Sophie knew she was wise to limit their time together. His kindness had reminded her of another life, one where she had been more petted and indulged than she'd realized. Yet she knew that there could be no more of it, no matter how tempting it would be to believe herself returning to that life. Better not to grow too accustomed to having her wants tended to with such miraculous ease.

Drawing rein at a crossroads, she asked him which way they were to go. Dominic stopped beside her. "You shouldn't ride too far today. You don't want a reoccurrence of your difficulties."

"No, indeed. I've learned my lesson. It's nice to shake out my fidgets, though, after two days in the carriage. I feel sorry for the maids. They have no choice in the matter."

"Are they unhappy?"

Sophie could not even imagine what technique he might employ to make two maidens so far from their home happy. For that matter, how far would he go to make her happy? Had that been his motivation for his proposal three years ago? She hadn't thought she was unhappy, not then. What had he seen?

"Oh, they will be very delighted to reach Finchley. I've told them about my mother and they are looking forward to meeting her, though a little apprehensive as well."

"Does she know they are coming?"

Sophie bit her lip and met his eyes with a glint of mischief in her own. "She knows I'm bringing one girl back from Rome, but the second, as I told you, was a surprise to me."

"What do you think she will do?"

"Cope splendidly, or so I imagine. Mother is very good at coping with all our troubles. Though I always thought it was Maris who caused the most worry. I never wanted . . ." There she went, spilling her intimate thoughts again. The only thing to do was shut her mouth tight, even biting her lip to keep the words dammed up.

"My mother has refused to come live with me, you know. Most people think she is dead."

"Why on earth would they think that?"

"She sent only her affidavit, testifying to my parentage." He tapped his heels against the sides of his horse and started moving off. Sophie followed, realizing the two coaches had paused rather than passing them at the crossroads.

"Were you disappointed that your mother didn't come to speak to the lawyers herself?" she asked, catching up.

He shook his head. "Mother does what she can."

"Is she unwell?"

"No, not physically. But her strength isn't all it should be. She simply could not withstand a journey from York to London."

"York? I visited there once when I was ill. The air is so wonderfully bracing."

"Yes, isn't it? Mother went to live with an aunt there after I went away to school. She hated relying on Great-Aunt Clementina's charity, and that's neither more nor less than what she offered."

Sophie would not have thought his good-natured face could look so bleak. For the first time, she wondered if the man behind the smile was more complex than she ever would have guessed.

"I can understand the wish to find a safe harbor, even if one must accept charity to find that security."

"Yes, I suppose that's what she did. She was worried

about me, too. Great-Aunt Clementina paid my school fees. In return, she demanded Mother's services as a companion, secretary, and general dogsbody."

"So she did it all for you?"

"Exactly."

"If I know women," Sophie said, riding knee to knee with him, "I'll lay odds she feels no regrets about her choices."

"None that she has ever mentioned."

"Would she?"

His lips twisted wryly. "Probably not."

"And you are a great man now, a noble, a man of wealth . . . have you given her a palace by the sea with columns carved of chalcedony?"

His frown remained. "No. She won't take a thing from me. She says that as she didn't live the life of a duchess with my father, she won't be a dowager duchess with me. She is, of course, and the people of her town call her so. My great-aunt can't stand it. She has always been the grande dame of the town, and to have her despised companion suddenly elevated so far above her . . ." He grinned, a mocking devil in his eyes. "It makes up for a lot, I can tell you."

"Yes, I can imagine your feeling of vindication." How wonderful it would be to be able to give her mother all the elegancies of life. If Broderick's poetry ever gained the renown it deserved, she would pour a bucketful of golden coins into her lap. How her mother would laugh—and then, inevitably, she would cry.

She looked around, almost surprised to see she hadn't been transported by fairy wish to her own home. But the cold wind still tossed the bare-fingered trees and the hooves still clopped relentlessly over the hard dirt road. She freed a hand to tug her cloak closer to her chin. "I think I had better change to the carriage. I'm a little cold."

The early dark was drawing in when the weary cavalcade at last came through the main, and virtually only, street of Finchley. Sophie leaned forward to gaze hungrily at the once familiar sights of her home. The last slanting red beams of winter sun illuminated so many memories. She'd once known every stick, stone, and soul.

Glancing up, she saw that lantern light shone through the bright stained glass windows of the old church. She'd seen grander religious edifices, both the golden glory of St. Peter's Basilica and the enduring magnificence of the Pantheon. Once she'd even been to York Minster. None of these, however, spoke to her with the loving warmth that the sight of her own church brought to her, the place she'd been christened, that she'd adorned with flowers as a girl, where she'd married.

Though she looked about her, devouring the street with her eyes, she realized that all the citizens must be within their homes. Most of the laboring families would have eaten before dark set in, while the gentry would only now be seating themselves about the family table. Their lights glowed behind drawn curtains. Sophie had to restrain her greediness to see her friends again.

Then the weary but still valiant horses drew them quickly beyond the village, to the impenetrable dark of the fallow fields. The coach lamps hardly illuminated that!

Sophie found she didn't need light to find her way. She knew the place where the gravel spurted from under the wheels and how they had to slow perforce for the place where the road dipped down. She heard the splash of water striking the panels of the coach, there where the little stream crossed the road, flowing in all but the most frigid temperatures. Then the wind sounded especially loud as they came through the place where the linden trees grew, their branches threshing in the breeze.

Yet when they reached the point when they should have turned toward Finchley Old Place, the coach continued on. She knew now where they were going. She only wondered why. Had her mother taken to living with Maris and her husband? It didn't sound likely, but one never knew. People did change so. Suddenly, Sophie felt a little frightened, almost as if she were going to strangers. She tossed a few reassuring words at the two girls huddled together on the opposite seat.

After a few more minutes and despite the frigid air, Sophie forced down the window and looked out, leaning on the frame. The two girls protested, huddling into their cloaks. Sophie, however, had eyes only for the house ahead, brilliantly shining with every window alight.

Then the front door opened above the curving double staircase that ran down a full flight to the ground. Silhouetted against the streaming golden light were the three people she loved most in the world, the women slightly more than the man.

Sophie hardly waited for the carriage to come to a stop. She threw open the door and leaped down, never mind the folding step. Stumbling a little, ignoring a sharp pain in her ankle, she ran to their open arms.

Mrs. Lindel, as ever, functioned as the still center of a chaotic storm. She saw to it that the groom, coachman, and boys had their feet tucked under the kitchen table within ten minutes of their arrival, mugs of hot tea in their reddened hands, and a smell of hot roast beef filling the air. Sir Kenton's own people were looking after the horses and unloading the luggage.

At another table, several of the younger girls attached to the household sat creating a garland of greenery for the holiday decorations. Gilded nuts nestled next to sprays of holly ripe with berries. The two Italian girls who had followed Sophie stood watching. "*Per Natale*?" Lucia asked.

"*Non so ancora*," Angelina answered with a shrug.

One of the girls, an under-dairymaid by the look of her apron, glanced up and smiled. She scooted over on her bench, motioning for another girl to do likewise. Beckoning to Lucia, she patted the space beside her. "Come on, it's easy. We'll show you what to do."

With a glance at her sister, Lucia sat down. The dairymaid put a bunch of nuts into her hand. "You thread them on like this," she said, demonstrating. "That's right. Come on, you too." She pointed to the other empty space. The other girls muttered or giggled depending on their temperament but, whether from kindness or from being under the eye of authority, they welcomed the Ferrara girls despite the language barrier. Sophie had every confidence they'd soon overcome that.

At a touch from her mother's hand, Sophie followed her. "Now, Sophie," she said, pausing in the gray-blue hall between servant's hall and the upstairs. "Tell me about those two young girls you have brought with you."

"They are very dear creatures. So patient and kind, with never a word of complaint through all the vicissitudes of this long trip." After a moment's thought, she added, "They are very hard workers, as well."

"But what are they doing here? Don't mistake me, pray. I am not objecting to their arrival. But I don't know what to do with them. We don't need two maids."

"I had to bring them both, Mother. I hadn't any

choice. Signora Ferrara could have thrown me on the street and kept all my clothes and furniture if I hadn't."

"But why on earth?"

"Because I couldn't pay her for my rent over the last three months."

"Why couldn't you? Did Broderick leave you so little?"

Sophie drew a deep breath. This was the most difficult part of her homecoming. "I have his poems."

"I see." Her mother's hair had grown slightly grayer, a few more lines had appeared in face and throat, but her eyes retained their faraway look. As usual, when those eyes sharpened and focused, her daughter could hold nothing back.

"He left me some eighteen months ago," Sophie murmured. "His mistress took everything when he died. His lawyer, misunderstanding the situation, told her before he told me. She took everything, his clothes, his books, his cravat pins . . . everything. But she didn't want his work, I suppose. It had no value to her. She'd thrown them down in the middle of the floor. There was a footprint on the top one." Sophie crossed her arms over her stomach, holding hard, trying to suppress the interior shaking that started whenever she thought about Catherine Margrave.

Mrs. Lindel reached out and drew Sophie into her arms. "Oh, my love," she said softly. "What has the world done to you?"

"It's not the world," Sophie said, her eyes tight against her mother's shoulder. "It would be easier to bear if I could say that. Then it would just be circumstances and one can't kick very much against circumstances. This was my own doing, Mother. All my own."

"Now, how can that be?" She took a step back, so to

look into Sophie's eyes, smoothing back the loosened hair from her flushed face.

"I married him, didn't I? Everyone told me I shouldn't. You, my uncle, even Dominic Swift warned me. But, no, I had to be stubborn. I was in love."

"Yes, you were. So radiant. Like a dancing sparkle on the water."

"They don't last, either." Sophie slipped out of her mother's arms and paced. "And Broderick's love for me lasted about as long."

"But what happened?"

"I don't know," she said, and all the agony of her confusion rang in her voice. "I tried to be a good wife. Every day I tried. We found an apartment right away, but there was nothing in it. So I went to the secondhand furniture shops—there are so many in Rome. I found wonderful things for just a few soldi. A table, a settee, a . . . a bed. I left them for Signora Ferrara anyway, as it turned out. They weren't worth taking back to the secondhand shops after . . . they weren't even worth the cartage."

If she closed her eyes, she could still see her apartment. She'd distempered the walls in a biscuit color soon after they'd moved in, but the leaks in the roof had mottled the walls into myriad tones. No matter how often she dusted and swept, a fine layer of silt would appear, softening colors and blending patterns. Every piece of furniture represented hours of searching, practicing her bad Italian until she'd bring home her hard-won prize.

At first, Broderick had enjoyed the expeditions as much as she. It was he who had chosen the funny little demi-lune table, decorated all over with birds in golden paint. They'd gotten it for an 'old song' he said, because one of the bun feet was broken in half, yet it had still been far more than they could afford. He'd laughed at the price, saying that their little nest needed some birds.

Sophie blinked back tears, refusing to cry over painted birds when she'd hardly shed a single tear for her late husband. She'd cried enough over him when he was alive, she decided. "I thought I was doing what he wanted. I made certain there was always something to eat in the house. I was quiet when he wanted to . . . to write, and I talked to him when he wanted conversation. But he didn't want a wife."

"What on earth did he want then?" Mrs. Lindel asked indignantly.

"A muse, I suppose. Someone who cared as little about regular meals or paying creditors as he. He found his muse in the mistress of an artist friend of his."

"So Broderick betrayed him, too?"

"Hamish didn't seem to mind so much. I suppose he'd found out what she was really like. It was only after Broderick took up with her that he started telling me to ask Uncle Shirley for money. Besides, Hamish had fallen in love with the French girl who used to model for him, his wife's second cousin. She was French, too, and had gone off with some count or other, Russian, I think, though he might have been Polish."

With a glance, Sophie saw that this last revelation had been perhaps too shocking. Mrs. Lindel had her hands up to her cheeks, her mouth agape. "What sort of horrible people did Broderick introduce you to?"

"Oh, there were many people who were much, much worse. Six months ago, I met a poet who'd run off with his wife's sister and was traveling through Italy with her and his wife and his wife's new paramour, who was a poet also, as well as all their multitude of children. They seemed very satisfied with the arrangements."

"Horrible, immoral people."

"I quite liked the sister, though she suffered from melancholia. Couldn't stand the poets. I suppose I had had too much of the artistic point of view by then."

"So I should think. Thank God you are home now among decent, well-bred folk."

"Oh, Mother, I do. I never thought I should see England again with or without Broderick."

"You should have written to me about all this. I had no notion your situation was so dire. If I had, I should have come to Italy myself to bring you home."

Sophie clasped her mother's hand. "I know, my dearest. That's why I didn't write. I couldn't bear for you to worry, being so far away. No, I had resolved to stay in Rome so long as I was married to Broderick. I knew we could never afford a divorce proceeding and, even if we could have, to be so gossiped about would have been torture for both you and me."

"Dear me, I hadn't thought of that."

"So long as I was so far from here and living among a set of people whom no English tourist ever sees, I could hide what had happened. Once he was dead, there was no need. I'm a respectable widow now. No one ever need know what a miserable failure my marriage was."

"Rest assured, no one will ever hear one word of this from me. I won't even tell Maris."

"No, indeed. She's so happy, isn't she?"

"Yes, she is. Dear Kenton worships the ground she walks upon and now that she is expecting their first child, well . . . you can imagine."

"Yes. Tell me, have they passed through that sticky phase when they were kissing in corners every minute?"

"Not yet, I'm afraid. One must always cough before entering a room here at Finchley."

"That reminds me," Sophie said. "Why are we here instead of at home? Are you living here now?"

"Heavens, no. I'm having the lower rooms painted and the ceiling in the dining room replastered. I wrote you, I think, that a whole corner fell during my dinner party in September?"

"Did it? The last letter I had from you came in July and was dated in May."

"Oh, of course. Well, anyway, Colonel McMullen was all but brained. I had no notion that a water jug over-turned in my room would cause such a disaster. Fortunately, the Cosbys have a cousin who does paint-ing and plastering. He was staying there while he worked. He's all finished now, but the house is in such disorder that Maris invited me to stay until the Cosbys come home. They went to visit their niece while the house was in disarray."

"How long before we can go back?"

"The Cosbys are coming home just after the New Year. If it were up to me, I should prefer to go home, but Maris and Kenton are pressing me to stay over Christmas. Of course, if you want to go back to Finchley Old Place, I will go with you. The two of us should be able to manage the housework."

"To be honest, I should like to draw out this period of luxury as long as I can, Mother. I have had enough of doing for myself."

"So I see by your hands," Mrs. Lindel said, taking the cold reddened hands into her own. "I have a pair of chicken-skin gloves I will lend you. Rub goose grease well in for a week and sleep every night in the gloves and soon your hands will be as white and lovely as before."

"I'm afraid I've forgotten all such secrets," Sophie confessed. "I'd like to stay on over Christmas. You have no idea how I have longed for an English Christmas. The Italians celebrate so differently."

"I do hope those girls won't feel too strange here. You say they speak no English."

"A few words only."

"Well, I'm sure I shall make myself understood. You go and take some dinner. I'll see to the girls."

"You don't want me to come along and translate?"

Mrs. Lindel shook her head. "I must be able to communicate without you. You won't always be about."

Sophie wondered where her mother thought she would be except at home. She'd learned her lesson. Hard taught, yes, but less likely then to be forgotten. Her future might contain many things. Love would not be among them. Never again.

CHAPTER FIVE

"Come on, Dom," Kenton murmured, glancing over his shoulder at the women huddled together on three armless chairs, discussing changes in the village with great intensity. Every now and again, laughter rang out, bright against the background of hushed voices. "Brandy in the library."

"Brilliant thought," Dom said. He sighed happily after one sip. "Wonderful stuff. You must introduce me to your smuggler."

"Quite legally acquired, actually. Half the profit is gone from smuggling now that the wars are over."

Dominic settled himself in a leather armchair, the twin of the one that Kenton sat in. At Finchley, they kept the civilized custom of dressing for dinner even when *en famille*, and Dominic wondered why his own black coat did not fit nearly so well as Ken's, even though they went to the same expensive tailor. He slid down onto his tail, his long legs up on a convenient footstool, his feet toward the fire.

At ease, he asked himself what more any man could need than a comfortable chair, an excellent glass of wine, and a good friend. A scratch and whine at the door made him peer around the swooping arm of his chair. The door swung open and a black dog with a milk-white tip to his long tail trotted in, a bright inquiry in his eye as if asking if he, too, might sit in the bow window at White's.

"Down, Tip," Ken said as the dog came forward to take a fascinated sniff at Dom's hand.

"He's a nice old chap, isn't he?" Dom said, reaching around lazily to tug at a silky ear, giving much gratification to its owner.

"Not good for much, I'm afraid," Kenton said. "Maris spoils him, and I've seen the servants slipping him bits of bacon when nobody's looking." Tip went to his master and lay down, his paws delicately crossed at the wrists.

Dom relaxed once more into the embrace of his most comfortable chair. The firelight flickered on the mellow leather spines of old books. The mulberry red curtains blocked the cold so well that one could almost forget the winter. Both men and dog sighed with bone-deep contentment.

"Now you can tell me the truth," Ken said. "Was it a very difficult trip?"

"I told you the truth already. There was nothing to it. Sophie fell in with whatever I suggested and never complained about a thing."

"Well, she wouldn't, would she? Not with you playing King Cophetua and the Beggar Maid over every mile. Good God, man, you bought her a horse!"

"For my pleasure. If you had seen her eyes when she talked about how long it had been . . ."

"I don't doubt the necessity. I'm only at a loss to know how to convince you to let me reimburse you for it."

Dominic chuckled. "I'll cut the cards with you later. High card pays."

"Done. I'll keep her here for Sophie. The stables at Finchley Old Place are rather a disgrace. One couldn't put a well-bred little mare like that in such a place."

"Well, repair them. You are the landlord."

"Only at a peppercorn rent. I don't fancy charging my mother-in-law for the whole amount."

"No, indeed. She might choose to save the rent by moving in here."

"She'll be here often enough once the baby comes. Maybe we should ask her to make her home here. Then I could rent Finchley Old Place to some new tenants."

"Or to Sophie."

"Sophie? It's a thought."

"No more money for you, though she might pay you out of pride. She is proud."

"It runs in the family," Kenton said with a reminiscent smile. "It can work in your favor if you know what to do."

"Oh, indeed?" came a woman's voice, full of both pride and laughter. "If you are giving instruction, my lord, may I sit at your feet?"

Maris Danesby waved to them to keep their seats. She perched on the arm of her husband's chair. His arm came up around her waist to support her.

Though one was not supposed to notice such things, Dominic rather thought that even in the two weeks he'd been gone her figure had changed. The child was not due to make an appearance for a minimum of two more weeks. However, women's fashions were not designed to hide fecundity.

Even more than the changes of body, a new glow had come into her face, a sense of peace that seemed to spread around her like the ripples in a pond. Ken had some of that quality as well. They seemed so satisfied in their union that nothing of rancor or vexation could survive against it. Dominic, taken aback by the surge of jealousy that swept over him, couldn't look at them. He addressed himself to his brandy, letting the aromatic heat burn the feeling away.

He had to force a smile as he looked up. After he met Maris's concerned eyes, though, the smile became more natural. His friend could have so easily married a horrible girl. Others of his friends had done so. Though Maris was quite young, she had a balanced view of life. Unlike other brides, she'd never interrogated Dominic about her husband's past life or the women appertaining thereto.

"I can't tell you how grateful I am to you for taking the time to escort Sophie home. It is as though I had the brother I always wanted."

Dominic saw Ken give Maris a tiny head shake. Her smile became even more innocently beatific. "Well, I shall leave you two to your drinking."

"We won't carouse too long or late. Dom looks tired."

"Did you really ride all the way from Dover? Wouldn't Sophie let you ride inside?"

"The weather was good so I never asked," Dominic answered. "I don't get enough exercise anymore. It's not like the old days when I would have walked from Dover to London. I should be the most ungrateful dog alive if I complained."

Tip opened a lazy eye upon hearing the word "dog." Seeing that nobody was offering him any food, he went to sleep again.

Dominic put his glass down on the table at his elbow, then stretched, one fist out, the other by his head. "I am tired."

Now Kenton shook his head at his friend. "You'll never send the polite world mad after your particular style of coat until you have it made tight enough to pop seams when you stretch."

"True, true. But what would you? I care more for comfort than for a neat appearance."

"For that, who can blame you?" Maris asked rhetorically. "I had thought men would forget all notions of dandyism upon marriage, but I have been sadly disillusioned. Kenton becomes more occupied with his attire with every season that passes."

"I strive only to be a credit to you, my love."

"Indeed you are." She leaned down and kissed him on the forehead. Then, a trifle awkwardly, she stood up and left the room.

"I don't know if I should warn you or not, Dom," Kenton said after a few minutes.

"Warn me?"

"When a wife gets that matchmaking gleam in her eyes, all a husband can do is hide in the library and suggest his friends do the same."

Though Dominic fancied his posture became no less relaxed, inwardly he felt an increase in tension. He took up his glass before he spoke. "Who is the fortunate female Maris has in mind for me? Some friend from the village?"

"No. Who else but Sophie?"

The ringing of the crystal as Dominic's glass bounced gently on the carpet was like the muffled ringing of fairy bells, soft but very clear in the paneled silence of the room. "It's all right," Dom said, leaning forward to pick it up. "The glass was quite empty."

Sophie was sitting up in bed, plaiting her hair before retiring, when the knock she expected sounded at her door. Maris popped her head in. "May I come in and talk to you? Or are you too tired?"

"No, I'm not tired at all." Under the covers, she

moved her legs over to make room. *Curious,* she thought, *we are so different, yet no one could mistake us for anything but sisters.* Their coloring was the same and their noses. Maris's hair was a deeper gold, her eyes a brighter blue. Though she'd put on some weight, naturally enough, her face hadn't changed very much. It retained the piquant interest in everything that had always been her leading characteristic.

Sophie, younger and shorter, couldn't help comparing their lives as well as their appearances. One had an adoring husband, a child on the way, a place in the world that was hers irrevocably. She would remain Lady Danesby until the end of her days. For herself, she had a dead husband, no children, no place except that of a fallen leaf, wafted by a wind into a river, there to float unmemorably until sunk. At most, she would rate a footnote in some future writer's history of Broderick Banner's brief life and tragically early demise.

Maris had by now absorbed the details of Sophie's appearance. "Do you have your dressing gown on? In bed?"

"And my thickest knitted bed socks and two petticoats."

"But it's quite warm in here," Maris said, glancing at the fireplace with a housewifely eye.

"Would you believe I'd quite forgotten how beastly the winters are in England? When I think how I used to complain when the temperature would fall to forty!"

"I suppose your blood became rather thin living there. But think of all the lovely sunshine in the summer. We had nine wet days in a row in the middle of June." She sat down on the edge of the bed.

"I'm hard to please," Sophie confessed. "I always found the summers too hot." She didn't add that it was because her stuffy little room never felt a breeze and all the heat from the stoves, along with all the torturing smells of good Italian cooking, collected there. "But enough of my nonsense. Tell me about you. What does Dr. Richards say?"

"About what one would expect. Stay quiet, no violent exercise, drink milk. How tired I am of milk!"

"But all is well?"

"So far as anyone can tell. What I hope is that once the baby is born, people will start fussing over it and not me. Between Mother and Ken, I hardly dare move without one or the other of them reminding me I should sit down."

"Everything is prepared, then?"

"Prepared and overprepared. One would think I was expecting the Heir of England," Maris said, then broke off, her eyes shadowed.

Though it had been three years and more since Princess Charlotte had died in childbirth, her fate hung like a sword over the heads of young women. She'd had the best attendants, the most famous obstetrician in England, Sir Richard Croft, to deliver the child—everything, in short, suitable for the Heiress of England. She had perished nonetheless, and the child with her. The Regent had been inconsolable. The unfortunate doctor had committed suicide a year and half later, despite being absolved of all blame in the case. If such wealth and care had brought about so grievous an outcome, what chance did lesser women have?

"By all I have heard," Sophie said, hoping to give her sister's thoughts a more cheerful direction, "men do behave as if a baby were all their own doing."

"Indeed, yes," Maris said. "A rooster crowing his own glory is nothing compared with it. The number of waistcoat buttons that I have sewn on is incalculable, his chest swelled so with pride."

"And you are no less excited about it, or so I gathered from your letter."

Maris leaned against the bottom post of the bed. "I was excited at the beginning. And I daresay I shall be excited once more at the end. But the months in between, my dear! So lengthy. So dull. One is advised not to ride. We went to Brighton. One is advised not to bathe. We went to London. One is advised not to dance. One mustn't read any invigorating literature for fear of the harm it might do the developing mind. Improving books only—and a duller occupation I should be hard-pressed to find. I could go to the theater, thank God, but only until my condition began to be apparent. A woman of quality, it seems, is never glimpsed when she is increasing."

"Poor Maris!"

"Poor Ken! I'm afraid I've not been the easiest person to please, and he tries so hard, the poor darling."

"He doesn't seem to be suffering too much," Sophie said, recalling how her brother-in-law paid the closest attention to his young wife, so much so that Maris's cup was filled almost before it was empty and she never need stand up without his hand at her elbow. Then, too, there was the look in his eyes when he gazed at her, that brilliant light of love that had gone out so soon in Broderick's eyes.

As if thinking of him brought him into her sister's mind as well, Maris suddenly spoke his name. "You never did tell us what happened to Broderick. Only that one letter informing us that he had died suddenly. Were you . . . with him?"

Sophie hesitated. Though it would relieve her mind to discuss the facts, she didn't know if it were right to burden another. If reading an exciting book might alarm an unborn child, what could a tale of sudden death do?

"Sophie?"

Of course, Maris did have, and always had, a wonderfully adventurous mind. Though she'd been destined for the quiet life of a gentleman's daughter, she'd won a grand prize in the Matrimonial Stakes—a wealthy, titled gentleman, the catch of the county. She'd done it by taking risks that would have terrified a professional gamester and, in the end, by laying her cards on the table without fear. Sophie couldn't imagine that her child would be any less intrepid.

Sophie leaned her head back against the upholstered headboard. "He took a trip to Sicily to edit his poems. A friend of his, Mr. Knox, accompanied him. Broderick was very fond of appreciating beauty firsthand. A few weeks after they arrived, Broderick fell down a rocky scree. He was picked up dead."

"Oh, my . . ." Maris groped for her sister's hand. She pressed it between her own, tears springing to her eyes. "You must have been devastated."

"He'd left me long before. All the same, I suppose I was appalled by the waste of his gifts more than any thing else. This is a great age for poetry and I believe, truly and even now, I believe he could have been the greatest of them all."

"Will you forgive me if I say I don't see him like that?"

"Of course," Sophie said with an inviting smile. "How did you see him?"

Looking off into the distance, Maris opened her mouth. Glancing suddenly at her sister, she shut it tight, her lips nearly disappearing.

"No, it's all right. I want to know."

"He didn't seem a very serious man," Maris said slowly. "Serious about anything. Not even on his wedding day."

"Oh, I think he loved me then."

"But not later?"

"No. Not by the time he was dead. Not for a long time before then."

"I don't understand."

"It's easy enough. He thought he loved me enough to be married to me. He didn't love me enough to live with me day after day, doing all the simple, ordinary things that husband and wife do for and with each other." Sophie was surprised by the sudden stab of pain she felt. Surely there must come a day when she either stopped producing pain or stopped feeling it. Someday, this wincing flesh must be covered by a scar—an ugly remembrance of agony, but no more than a dead region in her heart.

"I didn't mean that. I don't understand how you can be so calm about it. If Kenton ever left me . . ." The pink in her cheeks failed completely just imagining it, her hand creeping up to press against her heart.

"What should I have done? Murdered him? Jumped off Trajan's Column?"

"Did you cry?"

"Oceans. Atlantic, Pacific, Indian, Red Sea, Black Sea, bays, lakes, and rivers." She had no tears now. "I begged him on my knees to stay with me, not to abandon me in a strange country. He only laughed and told me he had fallen in love with someone else. He couldn't do anything about it, he said. He said that people couldn't be expected to control their feelings when feelings were, by their nature, the masters of reason and will."

"How horrible. To talk philosophy at such a moment. It's inhuman."

"I don't think he meant to be cruel. Or perhaps he did

but only to make as clean and sharp a break as possible. Perhaps he thought it would be less painful that way."

"You are far too forgiving. How can you even bring yourself to consider his feelings? It's absurd."

She lifted her hands and let them fall. "He's dead, Maris. Whatever crimes he committed against me, he is absolved."

"By you, if you like. But I am older than you and can hold a grudge for much longer. I shall pray tonight that God will let me forgive him, eventually."

Sophie slipped her hand free from her sister's grasp and returned to braiding her hair, changing the subject abruptly. "I've so looked forward to sleeping on a really good mattress. My bed in Rome was straw-stuffed and slung on ropes. Old ropes."

"You stayed at some very good inns, if I know Dominic. He isn't one to suffer from the inconveniences of inexpensive inns."

"To tell the truth, I'm quite glad the trip is over. I was in a fair way to becoming the most hideously spoiled child. If you'd sent a fairy godfather to look after me, I couldn't have been more spoiled."

Maris traced around the line of white knots that made up the pattern in the coverlet. "Do you . . . I mean you do like Dominic, don't you?"

"Naturally. I've always liked him. That is, for as long as I've known him, I've liked him. He has the rare quality of silence. He is almost dangerously easy to talk to. Now, why are you smiling?"

"He is Kenton's dearest friend. Of course I wish for you to like him."

"Then you have your wish," Sophie said lightly.

"And if I wished . . . never mind."

"Don't worry about me. You have more than enough to concern yourself with right now."

"True, but that will be over soon. I can go on worrying about you even after two more weeks pass."

"Then you'll have a baby to worry over. You concentrate on her."

"Her? Do you know something that I do not?"

"Wouldn't you like a girl? Honestly, now. Wouldn't you?"

"Between the two of us, and with the door closed, I'll tell you." She glanced over her shoulder. "I do not know what I should do with a boy."

"I remember how terrible we thought all boys were when you and I were children."

"Dreadful, noisy things. Always covered in dirt. In truth, men are very little different than boys. Of course, I should love it no matter what. A nice little girl, though, as nice as we were . . ."

"You were nice, Maris, and still are, though I seem to remember a girl falling off a horse and coming in covered with dirt and straw. And I wasn't much better. Do you remember when I fell out of the big oak and you carried me home because both my knees were bleeding?"

"Are you trying to tell me that my daughter will be a horrible little hoyden just as we were?"

"Just reminding you that not all little girls are prim princesses who sit happily sewing samplers."

"Heavens no, I forgot what a wretched hellion I was." Maris laughed. "Father liked us to be quite, quite fearless and we were, weren't we?"

"Yes, we were fearless . . . then."

They fell silent for a moment, each busy with thoughts that ranged over both past and future. Maris spoke first, with determined lightness. "I always thought it very brave of you, Sophie, to marry and live in a foreign country. Now that I know how often you were alone, I have even more respect for you."

"I was never afraid, not even after he left me. Well, afraid that nothing would ever change. But not afraid of poverty or of the strangers I'd meet. What had I that anyone could steal? That is why it was so strange . . ."

"What?"

"A few days before I left, my rooms were broken into. 'Broken into' indeed. They yanked out the drawers, ripped up the cushions, even tore the pictures off the walls."

"My poor dear! That's why you told mother your furniture wasn't worth taking to the secondhand shops."

"That's why. Odd that so terrible a thing should have happened after so many quiet days, and just before I left. It's as though fate were confirming my decision. I couldn't have slept comfortably there ever again, not without hearing every creak as the criminals returning."

"Did they steal anything?"

Sophie smiled a little bitterly. "I had nothing whatever worth the stealing. My landlady thought that was why they ran riot—out of disappointment."

"Thank heaven you weren't at home when it happened."

"No, I was at home very little those last days. So much to be done." Truthfully, the attack on her home had proved to be an attack on all her memories. She'd been able to treasure a few happy ones there, like roses under glass domes, but once she'd seen the devastation left by brutal thieves, even the few happy memories left after Broderick's desertion had been smeared and blackened.

After a moment, Maris spoke again, very quietly. "I only wish that you could have had a child or two.

Wouldn't it be wonderful if we could bring our children up together?"

Sophie pressed her fingers against her eyes, hoping Maris would think she was feeling nothing more taxing than tiredness. Hard as she found it to be brave in the daytime, night brought a new kind of attack against her bastions. Then to have her sister throw a bombshell over the walls, breaking them all to pieces, brought tears to long-dry eyes.

"Sophie? Oh, don't."

"It doesn't matter," she said, sniffing, hoping she didn't sound as pathetic as she felt. "I daresay Broderick would have felt even more tied down and worried if we'd had a child than he did with just me to burden him. After all, a child needs prudence and consistency and he believed that those things were death to the creative urge."

"I'm about to say something very rude."

"Don't. He was what he was. If I'd had more sense, I wouldn't have married him. Since I didn't have any sense, I must take the consequences."

"But not for always. You'll marry again. Then you'll have a worthwhile man and children and happiness, all that you deserve."

"Of course," Sophie said, only to comfort Maris. In her present state, she wouldn't trouble her with the facts. Eventually, as the years passed, Maris would accept that her sister had no intention of taking that long leap in the dark a second time. By then, with luck, Maris would be so busy with a large family and all their troubles, in romance and without, that her eternally widowed sister would never impinge on her thoughts.

With visible and vocal efforts, Maris leveraged herself off the bed. "I don't know about you, but I simply crave some biscuits. There are some very special ones downstairs in the biscuit barrel. Mrs. Lemon might even make us cocoa, if we ask nicely. Want to come?"

"Goodness, yes, I'm absolutely starving."

CHAPTER SIX

The next morning, Sophie awoke to the perfect silence of a snowy morning. She knew, even before she went to the window, that a deep batting had fallen over all, muffling sound and lending all things a pristine beauty. She threw aside the covers and scurried across the frigid floor. Throwing open the drapes, she glanced out and saw that what she'd imagined had come true.

Standing on one foot, warming the other against her goose-pimpled calf, she gazed out with affection upon the garden. The fountain in the middle of the court looked like a tiered wedding cake with meringue-like swathes of snow hanging from the edges in the stillness of a windless morning. The stone cupid on the top looked very cold, with no covering save wings. His arrow pointed directly toward her window. Suddenly, absurdly nervous of that symbolism, Sophie stepped back, out of sight.

Quickly she skittered over the floor to the fireplace, the whitewashed wooden floor cold as marble under her feet. When she picked up the poker, it felt like an icicle. Nevertheless, she stabbed at the logs, banked and covered in black and ash, until a red glow awoke in the charred wood and flames began to revive. Then she fed it with a new log, nearly dropping it on her toes. Another jab with the poker and a bright blaze began to warm the room. Sophie watched it for a moment, to be sure all had caught, then made a flying run across the floor to burrow deep under her goose-feather coverlet once more.

She watched the flames reaching up as if to claw back and devour the cold as her cold feet sought for the flannel-wrapped brick in the depths. Its heat was long gone. Her eyelids began to drift closed again and she did not fight the sensation. When she awoke the second time, it was to the sound of the curtain rings shaking and the scent of tea. Tea!

Sophie struggled free of her enveloping covers, sitting up. A neatly mobcapped maid had her arms up as she adjusted the hang of the curtains. Another stood by, a supervising light in her eye, her hands full of a tea tray with a most intriguing set of covers upon it.

"Good morning, madam," this one said. "Did you sleep well?"

"Like a top," Sophie replied. "I made up the fire."

"Yes, madam. You should have rung."

"Oh, but it was so early. At least, it felt early. I don't think that clock is right," she added, pointing to the wooden-case clock on the mantel between two Chinese vases. It said half-past ten.

"I'll ask the butler to look at it, madam," the maid said as she set the tray across Sophie's knees. "Mr. Tremlow is a dab hand with a clock. Sets and winds them all himself."

The other maid, satisfied at last with the curtains, turned about. Sophie glanced at her discreetly, then stared. "*Che bella giornata,* Lucia!" she said.

The girl's large brown eyes flicked to the English maid. "Good . . ." she prompted.

"Good mor-ing, Signora Banner."

"Morn-ing. Morning."

Lucia gave one of those incredibly impressive shrugs by which a Roman says so much more than mere words can express. The English girl gave her own nation's contribution to silent scorn—an exaggerated eye roll.

Sophie called her back just before she closed the door. "What's your name?"

"Parker, madam," she answered, looking slightly worried.

"Parker, I want something from you."

"Madam?" Her vague worry solidified into an expression of considerable alarm, as if she were examining her conscience and finding it full of gaping holes.

"Could you imagine that you have just been dropped down in a strange country, where you hardly speak a word of the language and haven't seen a friendly face yet?"

"Madam?"

"Would you be very kind to that young lady and her sister? They have a hard time ahead of them just in learning English, let alone discovering all their duties."

"Yes, madam. Though that Angelina girl seems to understand more than this one does."

"Does she? Well, be kind to them, if you please. Don't laugh at them or make the mistake of thinking that because they speak no English that they must necessarily be fools. I'm sure that with your example, the other servants will follow along."

"Yes, madam," she said. Sophie was perfectly well aware that Parker couldn't very well have said anything else. However, she felt confident that some of her meaning had reached the maid.

After half an hour, Sophie trotted down the stairs, adjusting her shawl about her shoulders. She didn't see

Dominic until she all but ran into him at the bottom of the staircase.

His hands came up to fend her off, winding up catching her against his chest instead. For one instant, breathing in sharply, Sophie flushed with a remembrance that was more of the body than of the mind. She had the impression that she stared up at him like a frightened doe for a long time. In reality, it couldn't have been more than a second or two before he stepped away, his hands falling to his sides.

"You look, if I may say so, much more rested this morning."

"Is it still morning?"

"Well then, this afternoon." He offered his arm. Somewhat gingerly, Sophie took it, aware of the muscle beneath the sleeve. "I'm afraid you've missed church."

"Did I? I'm sorry to hear it. I was hoping to go but I was so very tired."

"So was I," he said. "I always sleep better in the country. So much quieter than town."

"Especially with the snowfall. What a delightful surprise for my first day here."

"I'm so happy you are pleased with it."

"Did you do it?" she asked with a smile. She remembered how she and Broderick used to joke like this, and her smile wavered like a flickering candle.

Dominic didn't seem to notice. "Of course. I'm on the best of terms with the snow elves."

"Snow elves?" Sophie almost laughed out loud.

"Absolutely. Didn't you know they make the snow? My good girl, what sort of upbringing have you had? Never heard of the snow elves?"

Sophie saw that the curtains had been thrown open along the far wall, disclosing a striped cushion set in a bow window seat. She walked toward it at once, to sit with her feet tucked up and her back against the wall. A breath of cold air poured along the window but the view was so marvelous down the snow-covered lawn that she couldn't resist sitting there. "I'm sadly ignorant of meteorology. It wasn't considered a necessary study for females."

"How unfair." He seated himself to lean against the other wall, his long legs over the edge of the cushion.

"Yes. For instance, I never knew elves controlled the weather. How shockingly ignorant you must think me."

"It's not your fault. Shall I teach you all about them? Maybe you can learn to see them if you study very hard."

"You must think me about ten years old, Your Grace."

"I? I assure you, quite the contrary." He had such bright eyes, with so penetrating a gaze that she could not meet it for very long. He made her very self-conscious. She could turn her head to gaze out the window whenever his gaze grew too concentrated for her to sustain.

"Let us speak seriously, if we can."

"If you wish, though I'd rather talk piffle, just to see you smile again."

"Oh, now that I'm home again, I'm sure I will smile a great deal. But what I wanted to ask you is this: Do you still have friends among writers?"

"Yes, quite a few. Some I even support with funds from time to time. Why? Are you thinking about your husband's poems?"

"I'm determined to see them published. I have no doubt that these are poems that will speak to thousands of men and women all over this country."

"You have such faith in your husband's voice?"

"Yes," she said, giving a short, decisive nod. "Any advice you can offer me will be most gratefully accepted.

I only know what Broderick himself told me about selling poems."

"What did he say?"

"That compared with selling a poem, writing one is easy."

Dominic chuckled. "He had a point."

"Do you miss it?"

"The struggle? No. I could sell anything now. I receive offers by every post, pleading with the Duke of Saltaire to grant them the opportunity to publish whatever I choose to send them. But they wouldn't look twice at the writings of Dominic Swift."

"So you don't write at all now?"

"Once in a while. When something strikes me as interesting or important."

Sophie leaned forward, resting her chin on her fist. "What do you find interesting and important?"

"People, mostly. Sometimes an idea or, more often, a fragment of an idea."

"Not poetry, though?"

"No, never poetry," he said, raising one hand as if taking a vow. "Just between us, I can't rhyme hat with cat."

"Broderick used to say that rhyme was too easily devolved into mere doggerel. He felt the future of poetry was in rhythm, not rhyme. Though, I must confess, he still clung to rhyme. He wrote a very pretty one once to the ribbons in my hair." Sophie tried to remember how it began.

Dominic cleared his throat rather stagily. "Of course, now is an excellent time to sell a collection of poems. Ever since Byron hit such a smite, all the publishers have been seeking the 'next Byron.'"

"Broderick had no opinion of Byron. He thought most of his lordship's popularity came from his appearance."

"Quite," Dominic said.

"It wasn't entirely jealousy," Sophie reassured him. "Broderick was handsome, but not in quite so showy a way."

"I suppose you must have thought him tolerably good-looking . . ."

"I admired him for his mind. I never thought of him in any physical way." Sophie felt her face heat and leaned back into her corner. What on earth had she just said? That moment when Dominic had held her, however accidentally, must have confused her more than she'd realized. She had only enough sense not to fuddle the issue further by making explanations or excuses. Let what she had said stand.

"A marriage of minds can be the most satisfying," he said sententiously.

Sophie tilted her head to study him. Did he believe that? "Would you settle for such a marriage?"

"We are not talking about me."

"No, of course not. Do you think . . ."

"However, as you mention the matter, no. Such a marriage would not satisfy any man who truly loved a woman. When I marry, I will choose a woman whom I desire on every possible level. I will cherish her, mind, soul, and body."

If she blushed before, it was no more than a tinge of pink on a white rose. She felt her face flame, yet managed a steady voice. "She will be a most fortunate woman. Do you think you will ever find such a one?"

"I live in hope."

Until that moment, he'd been sitting in one of his usual postures of all but boneless relaxation. Now, he straightened, a look of determination hardening his pleasant features. "My dear . . ."

Sophie turned her head to look out the window. A

strange excitement began to flutter behind her breast-
bone. "Is that the carriage I hear returning?"

"I don't know." He reached across to take her hand in
his own. Sophie had to look at him, perforce. "My dear,
will you let me help you?"

"Help me? How?"

"As you have asked. And more. I will help you edit
and sell those poems."

"You will? I confess I am dreading making some horrible mistake with them. Mr. Knox asked if I would
consider his aid, you know."

"Mr. Knox," Dominic repeated, releasing her hand.
"That fellow who sailed home with you?"

"Yes. He was Broderick's dear friend. He traveled
with him, visited him so often that he knew his thoughts
intimately."

"He sounds ideal. But you refused his offer of assistance?"

"I felt it wiser not to encourage the acquaintance. You
see . . . he claims that he wishes to marry me, and I simply cannot consider such a thing."

"You've had enough of poets."

"I've had enough of love."

A noise and bustle in the hall heralded the return of
the church party. Maris inquired of the butler where her
sister might be. Naturally, the butler knew.

Maris, still swaddled in her fur-lined robes, came in
and saw them sitting together in the window seat. "Here
you are," she caroled.

Sophie swung her feet to the floor and came to kiss
her sister and take her wraps. "Good sermon?"

"Excellent. I wish you could have heard it."

"So do I. Dr. Pike is always so inspiring."

"Oh, didn't Mother write you? The Pikes are no
longer in residence."

"Gone? I thought they were an institution." Sophie looked toward her mother for an explanation.

"Once their oldest boy left to be a teacher and took Lucy with him as a housekeeper, the vicarage was too big for the remaining family. Then Dr. Pike's health began to betray him. They are very happily settled on the Isle of Wight, of all places. For the sea air."

"I see. Who is vicar now?"

"A very nice man, Mr. Ward."

"Too charming to be a clergyman," Maris added. "You'll meet him this evening, if you feel up to it. I would have him here to dinner but I shouldn't be much of a hostess at the moment." She eased herself into the chair her husband had sat in the night before. "I don't mind a family party, but not neighbors. Not until after I'm churched."

Mrs. Lindel spent a moment making Maris more comfortable, then excused herself. From the doorway, out of Maris's sight, she beckoned to Sophie.

"Yes, Mother?"

"I was happy to let you sleep in, Sophie, but many of our friends were asking after you. Would you consider accompanying me on some calls in the next few days?"

"Certainly. I should be very happy to."

"Our friends have been most anxious about you since I told them of your husband's unfortunate passing. Yet, though I hesitate to mention it . . ."

"What concerns you, Mother?"

"Don't mention your troubles to anyone but me. Maris has done enough lately to shock the village."

"Maris? What can she have done?" Sophie asked, following her mother up the stairs.

"She insists, despite all my advice, in appearing in church even though her condition is so obvious. It shocks our friends, and everyone talks about her behind her back."

"Why? Don't they know where babies come from?"

"Sophie," her mother said with a laugh in her throat. "You mustn't say such things. Though you've been married, there are still things one doesn't discuss, especially when men are about. Maris will say things to dear Kenton that shock me, and I am not easily shocked. Not after your father."

She opened her bedroom door and led the way in. Mrs. Lindel untied her bonnet with the purple roses and laid it carefully on the hat form on her dressing table. As usual, her movements were always tidy, and everything about her room was tidy as well. Sophie realized how far she'd departed from her mother's standards, thinking guiltily of the clothes she'd left thrown on the bed and the clutter on her own dressing table. Mrs. Lindel had taught her daughters that while care could not replace fortune, neatness always made a young lady appear more desirable a friend.

"You would think, after Father's escapades and Maris's startling a larger world than Finchley with her marriage, that our friends would have grown accustomed to the Lindels' unconventional ways."

"People are always willing to be shocked anew. If you could but suggest to Maris that she stay at home."

"Why should she listen to me? I'm the younger sister."

"I know she respects your mind and your wider experience of the world."

"I'm sorry, Mother. My wider experience tells me nothing about being a mother. Not even an incipient mother."

"Still, you must see why it's so startling. She is very near her time. When I was in such condition, I stayed inside and quite out of sight."

"Didn't you feel confined?"

"That is why they call it a confinement, my dear."

Sophie shook her head, more at her own folly than at her mother. "I'd forgotten. I will speak to her. However . . ."

"However?"

Sophie tried to think of a way to be subtle. "You do realize the problem will be solved in a week or so anyway."

"Yes, that's true. That's one reason why I want her to stop gallivanting about. She never seems to take any rest."

"Yesterday . . ."

"Oh, she lies down upon her bed, but she doesn't spare herself. I know she walks the halls at night when she should be sleeping. Dear Kenton is at a loss. All he can do is walk with her." She sat heavily on her bed, a cardinal sin in her philosophy. "I'm afraid for her," she said almost to herself.

Sophie came to her side and sank down on the floor at her mother's feet. "It's been very difficult for you. I'm sorry for my part. I will try not to add any more to your worries."

Her mother's hand lightly stroked the smooth hair on top of her head. "When you have children, trouble and worry are hardly unexpected. Never think that I am not proud of both my girls. Your father would have been proud of you, especially."

"Would he?" Sophie asked. It was rare for her mother to do more than speak of her late husband except in passing. All Sophie really knew of him was that he'd been a bruising rider, a man of little tact and much good humor. She could remember him well, for he hadn't died until she was twelve. But there would always be a wide gap between a woman's knowledge and a child's.

"Yes. He never had time for people who wept over ill

fortune. He would have been so proud that you didn't beg for help when Broderick left you."

"I wept a great deal, Mother."

"I'm sure you were courage itself. Just like your father."

Mrs. Lindel encouraged Sophie to stand up and swept her with an all-encompassing glance. "We must do something about your clothes."

"They aren't really so bad," Sophie said. "They are only three years old. It's just that I lost a little weight."

"How much?"

"I've no idea."

Her mother rose to her feet and came over to tug the back of Sophie's morning gown tight against her figure. "My goodness, there's five inches to take in here if there's one. I'll have to look over your clothes, see which ones are worth altering. You can still sew?"

"Of course. I altered a few things at first. Later, there was just so much to be done, I'm afraid I fell behind."

A rap at the door behind her made Sophie turn while her mother looked around and smiled. Maris came in. "Are you talking to her about her clothes?"

"You too?" Sophie said without surprise.

"I'm sorry, dear, but they are simply appalling."

"You haven't seen them all." Sophie felt herself grow defensive and realized, with an inward smile, that there was no need. They were completely right; her dresses were appalling. "Most of my shoes are half-soled or re-heeled, as well," she admitted, surrendering to forces too strong for her.

"My feet are too swollen to fit in my shoes, so that's one problem solved. As for my dresses, I think even they would have to be altered to fit you now."

Considering that Maris was two inches taller and

much more slender prior to her pregnancy, her gowns would certainly need alteration.

"There's nothing for it," her mother said resignedly. "We shall have to visit Finchley first thing tomorrow. I shall send a note to Miss Bowles that she should expect us no later than half-past ten o'clock."

"Miss Bowles?" Sophie echoed. "I thought . . . didn't you always insist that we make our own clothing? What happened to the material and such stuff that you had put aside?"

Her sister and her mother exchanged glances. "Sophie," Maris said with a tinge of pity, "we are not poor anymore. There's no need to prick our fingers over such work. Miss Bowles needs the money we pay her far more than we need to save it."

Sophie stepped away from them. "I cannot accept a wardrobe from your husband, Maris."

"Why not? You accepted a whole horse."

"That was an excess of generosity on the part of His Grace. Besides, I consider that horse belongs to him, not to me. I only had the use of it. Clothes, however, are a different matter."

Again a glance passed between Mrs. Lindel and her eldest daughter. "They wouldn't be from Kenton," the older woman said. "They would be Maris's Christmas gift to you."

"From my pin money," Maris added.

"Your pin money? You can't spend that on me. It isn't right. That's for your use alone."

"What else am I to spend it on? Since my marriage, I've not been allowed to spend a shilling on myself. Kenton pays for all. I haven't seen so much as a single bill. He takes them all before I can even see the totals."

"That's very generous."

"Ah, yes," Maris said, sighing ecstatically. "Kenton is

the best of men, the kindest of husbands, the most delightful . . ."

"Maris." Mrs. Lindel cut her off quickly but indulgently.

Maris looked down and smiled a little shamefacedly. "I'm afraid I become a little carried away."

Sophie came back to her side. Passing her arm about her sister's enlarged waist, she gave her a hug. "You deserve all the happiness in the world. I have always thought so."

"What a picture," their mother said. "If I were an artist, that is the image I should wish to capture. My girls, all grown up but still as close as ever."

Now it was Sophie's turn to meet Maris's eyes. When Maris raised her eyebrows, she gave in, though she didn't feel entirely comfortable with that acceptance. "Thank you, Maris, if you are certain Kenton won't object."

"Good. Mother, she doesn't have to wear mourning, does she? It would be such a shame."

"Dear me, I hadn't considered. She should, I suppose."

"Half mourning," Maris decreed. "White, gray, lilac. Pale shades offset with darker. We must show off her tiny waist and perfect complexion."

"Yes, that has possibilities. Perhaps add a fringe across her forehead."

"No, no," Maris said. "But lightly formed curls beside her ears would draw focus to her eyes."

"Perhaps. Certainly this manner of hair won't do at all."

"I beg your pardon," Sophie said, unsure whether to laugh or be indignant. "Am I to have nothing to say in all this?"

Though they both said reassuring things, Sophie realized that they weren't actually listening. Mrs. Lindel brought out some hoarded issues of *Ladies' Magazine*. Maris sat down in an armchair by the window, holding the books open awkwardly on her rounded stomach.

Though they referred to Sophie for her preferences as to decorations, they overruled her ruthlessly. Her taste leaned toward the simple, the straight-lined, and the discreetly covered. According to both Maris and Mrs. Lindel, these notions were hopelessly outmoded. Waists had begun to curve inward and approximate the natural. The absence of trimming and floss that appeared elegant to Sophie made Maris roll her eyes to heaven. As for covering, necks were lower than had been seen for several years.

Eventually, Sophie found the best thing to do was to slip away during the discussion of the suitability of certain hats considering her widowed state. Closing the door behind her softly, she blew out her breath, relieved at her escape. Her old dresses suddenly seemed more comfortable and desirable than they had in years.

Hearing a soft chuckle, she turned to see Dominic, dressed to go out, leaning against the wall several doors down the hall. Before she could speak to him, her mother's voice, muffled, came through the door. "Now, where did she go?"

Sophie cast him a half-laughing, half-desperate glance. "Hide me?"

He made a long arm and opened the door beside him. "Hurry."

CHAPTER SEVEN

Feeling more than a little foolish, Sophie waited in the silence of Dominic's bedroom. Though the bed was made and the room generally straightened, certain signs gave away that the occupant of the room was definitely male. A boot fallen over beside its comrade, a crumpled cravat on the bow-front bureau, a few loose notes scattered about, one having drifted to the floor, showed that Fissing was either gravely ill or no longer with his master.

Sophie occupied a few moments picking up the note and setting the boot to attention. Catching sight of herself, she peered into the dark-framed mirror, lit from the window, and wondered if her appearance truly was as dire as her mother and sister believed. Granted, her cheeks were rather pale. Perhaps she could use a trifle of rouge, just temporarily. And perhaps pulling her hair back so tightly did leave her looking more like an onion than was attractive, however practical it might be.

Pulling a few tendrils loose at her left temple, Sophie studied the effect, turning her head from side to side to judge the difference. When she tugged at the right side, however, one of her tortoiseshell pins slipped out, causing half her hair to tumble out of the double twist she habitually wore.

"*Mannaggia*," she said, irritated. With a glance over

her shoulder, she set about repairing the damage. Flicking out the rest of the hairpins, she combed her fingers through her long blond hair, smoothing out the kinks created by twisting damp hair first thing in the morning.

When Dominic tapped lightly at the door, she said, "A moment, please," but a pin she held between her teeth fell to the floor. She knew several other Italian imprecations, it being a language singularly well-stocked with invective, but she shut her mouth tightly to keep the other pin from following.

"Mrs. Banner?" Dominic poked his head around the door. His eyes widened and he glanced instinctively behind him. "What happened?"

"An attack of vanity," she said, jabbing a pin into the heavy mass. "Would you be very kind and pick up that hairpin?"

He went down on one knee to peer for the dark brown prongs against the deep red and blue figured carpet that ran under the bed. "I don't see it."

"It must have bounced." Holding one hand flat against the side of her head to keep the unsupported half of her hair from tumbling down around her neck again, Sophie bent down to look. "Maybe it went under the bed."

"Or the bureau." Despite his coat and shallow-crowned hat, Dominic went down on his stomach to reach a questing hand under the bureau. "Here it is," he said, pushing up with his arms. Again on one knee, he handed it to her.

Sophie heard a strange, choked sound from the hall. She didn't know if it was her mother, her sister, or one of the servants, but this was not the room or the company she wished to be discovered in with her hair down. "Thank you," she said, taking it from his hand and plunging it into the loops of hair all in virtually the same motion.

"What were you hiding from?" he asked, looking up at her curiously.

"Advice," she answered shortly. "Please, Your Grace, stand up before someone sees you like that."

His eyes laughed at her. It was hard to believe that his hand had once been hers for the asking. Sophie still wondered what had prompted his strange proposal the night before she'd married. Though it was useless to repine over the past, she couldn't keep from wondering what her life would be like now if she'd accepted him. Perhaps the scandal would have died down after three years. Impatient with herself, she turned about sharply to look in the mirror, checking that her hair and her complexion were both as usual. She'd made the right choice. She was never destined to be a duchess.

Dominic rose to his feet behind her. Sophie noticed that her head came to his shoulder, just the right height to lean against. The smile had gone out of his eyes. "Is it awkward for you, my remaining in this house?"

"No, certainly not. Why would it be?"

"There are certain passages between us, as you may remember."

"I remember," she said quietly. Then, rallying, she added, "Besides, if these considerations did not trouble you in Dover . . ."

"They did. I did not want to refuse a favor asked of me by my best friend, but I would rather not have gone to meet you."

"I remain grateful that you did. No one else could have made me so comfortable." Smiling with bright determination, she turned around, only to find that the mirror had deceived her. He stood very close behind her. "I hope you know," she said, lifting her hand to rest against the pulse beating in her throat, "that you have more than one friend under this roof, Your Grace."

His gaze rested on her lips, almost as if he were unable to hear her words. She'd not noticed before that his eyes were quite such a deep, clear blue, nor that there were tiny gold flames in their depths. Then his gaze lifted, and Sophie felt as if she'd been released from a spell.

"I wish to heaven you'd stop calling me that." He stepped back and Sophie drew a breath.

"What should I call you?"

"Dom, as Kenton and Maris do. Or Saltaire, as your mother does."

"All right. Saltaire. And you may call me . . . Mrs. Banner."

That brought the smile back. "Very well. Mrs. Banner, would you care to accompany me to the stables? I want to make sure our horses are well bestowed."

"Your horses," she said. "I should like that. I'll meet you downstairs in five minutes?"

"Excellent."

Sophie did not expect to be alone when she reached her room. She was not disappointed. "Tell me all," Maris demanded.

"I thought it was you. Were you eavesdropping?"

"Naturally."

"Marriage has had a bad effect on your moral fiber, I fear."

"Don't change the subject. What is between you and Dominic?"

"Tell me, what are you giving Kenton for Christmas?"

Maris's eyes sparkled. "I found the most wonderful man in Ludgate Street and I had him make a new microscope for Ken."

"A microscope? How interesting."

"All the pieces fit into the case like jewels. I'm sure he'll love it. He's still using the one he had at school, and they've improved out of all recognition since then."

"What does he use it for?"

"He's interested in all sorts of things, but mostly in classifying the parasites and mildew on his roses."

Sophie hid a smile. She never would have believed her sister or any woman could become rapt with interest over aphids and black spot. "It's important for a man to have an outside interest."

"Yes, indeed. Which brings me back to my earlier question." Maris stood up and tugged on the bellpull. "What interest does Dominic Swift have for you?"

"For me? None, I imagine. I am the sister-in-law of his best friend, that's all."

"What do you think of him?"

"He's charming," Sophie said lightly. "What else should one think of him?"

"Parker," Maris said to the maid who appeared in the doorway, "my good boots, please, the dark green ones. My sister is going out."

"The fur-lined cloak as well, my lady?"

"Yes, I think so. Thank you, Parker."

Sophie's pride slipped a little from its pinnacle when she saw how beautifully the cloak became her. The edge of marvelously soft brown fur caressed her chin while the deep green made her skin look like alabaster. Burying her hands in the matching muff of banded fur, she couldn't help feeling a little eager to see what Dominic would think of her dressed as a great lady, if only on the outermost layer.

She walked down the stairs, holding her head very high, only to find the lower landing was empty. Had she misunderstood?

Wasting a little time in the hall, Sophie admired the marble busts tucked into niches at intervals along the entry. She hadn't had time before to look at the beauties of Finchley. Though not the largest country house in England, everything was of the highest quality and the best of modern taste. The Danesby family had been wise in investments, being among the few who had escaped prior to the collapse of the South Sea Bubble, as well as choosing wealth over honors throughout their long history. Had their choices been different, Kenton might have a title as high as Dominic's.

She walked into the library, thinking he might be there. He wasn't. Sophie ran her finger along the spines of the books, admiring the gold crest impressed upon each one's leather. In between the towering bookcases, handsome if overvarnished portraits of former tenants of the house hung in gilt frames. A highly polished tall-case clock, decorated with marquetry scenes of old China, chimed sonorously.

The fire was leaping and she soon felt too warm in her sister's cloak. Retreating farther from the fire's reach, she bumped into a curly-legged writing desk with a leather top. Sophie turned and blinked with surprise.

On the oxblood leather surface she saw a papier-mâché box that she knew as well as she knew her own face. Painted to look like burled walnut, it rested on brass lion's paws with a dimensional mask of a lion centered on the top. His nose was slightly rubbed so that the underlying material showed through. She'd brought it from Italy, but what was it doing here? It should be in her room.

"Here you are," Dominic called from the entry. "I was in the kitchen, wheedling a few lumps of sugar from the cook. Are you ready to venture into the cold?"

"Quite ready." Sophie put out a hand to open the box. The lid stuck a trifle.

"That's a pretty thing. French, isn't it?"

With a little wiggling, the top rose on its hinges. A stack of tightly compressed papers sprang up in a soft explosion. Sophie laid a hand on them to keep them together. "Broderick always claimed it was Egyptian, that it had held the love letters of Anthony and Cleopatra. Nonsense, of course, just like his notion that it brought him good luck. He said that whenever he put a poem in this box, it would sell."

"So you've put them all there?"

"Yes. More for safekeeping than to invoke the power of the gods. Besides, I can't imagine anything of Cleopatra's would exactly breathe good fortune. She was unlucky in love *and* war."

"Did you want to start working on them right away?"

"Soon," she said. "Not immediately. To be frank, I'm in dire need of a little fresh air. It's pleasant to have roaring fires in all the rooms, so heavenly not to have to worry about keeping warm, yet they do make it a trifle airless."

"The stables await, madam," Dominic said with a half bow.

She smiled as she took his arm, yet couldn't keep from glancing back. "I just don't know how they came downstairs by themselves."

"I beg your pardon?"

"Nothing. I'm only curious to know who brought my box into the library."

"You didn't bring it here?"

"No. I left it in the drawer of my bureau after the maid unpacked for me."

"One of the servants must have brought it down. Someone probably overheard you talking about them. If

Fissing were here, we'd know who to blame. That man is 'no canny' as the Scots say. I believe, you know, that he reads my mind."

"Fissing impressed me as being unique."

"Like master, like man? I wish it were true, but I'm afraid I am a very ordinary man."

"But how can you say so?" she asked. "You have achieved a great position."

"Not by my own efforts, but by an extraordinary twist of fate. I didn't plan to be a duke's grandson; that was my father's fault entirely."

He led her to the rear of the library and opened the French doors which led to the loggia that ran the entire length of the back of the house. It was sheltered from the snow by a sloping roof supported on pillars that had an antique appearance. Though the air was still, the cold seemed to strike inward with every breath. Sophie huddled a little more deeply into her cloak.

"This way," he said, walking down the three steps to the ground. He held out his hand to her. Sophie took it, surprised by the warmth even through his gloves and hers. He smiled as if she'd done him a very great favor. "Carefully," he said, "there are sure to be icy patches."

"It's wonderful. So bracing."

"To say the least. Do you remember the winter of 1816?"

"Indeed. No spring, no summer, only cold, colder, coldest."

"I was living in a hovel on the cusp of Oxford Street in those days, buying old picture frames for pennies. Much cheaper than firewood."

She didn't believe him, but she laughed anyway.

The stables were some distance away down a crazy-paved brick path, behind a rise of ground. Beside it, like a palace of cloudy ice, stood Kenton Danesby's precious greenhouse, the greenery inside glimpsed through the befogged windows. There was something magical about a thriving colony of plants set down in the midst of winter, as if one would open the door not into a greenhouse, but into another world where it was still summer.

As he warned her, some of the bricks were filmed with ice. She took a stronger grasp of his arm. Despite that, a patch of ice overlaid with frozen leaves made her slip. She laughed a little and grabbed Dominic with both hands to keep from falling. The muff fell to the ground.

"All right?" he said, smiling down into her eyes. He bent to pick up what she'd dropped. She took it from him, sliding the warm puff halfway up her arm for safety.

"May I?" He wrapped his arm about her waist, giving her the support of his strength. The cobbled surface of the yard was equally treacherous, and Sophie was glad that she wasn't alone.

The dark stable smelled richly of horses and straw, overlaid with the smoke from the stove at the far end. The grooms stood up, putting down mugs of tea, reaching for their coats to cover their shirtsleeves. The head man, short, bandy-legged, but with arms banded with muscles, came forward.

"We're sorry to disturb you," Sophie said. "We just came to visit the horses."

"To be sure, ma'am. This way," he said, a tinge of Irish living still in his voice. He took down a pierced lantern from a nail by the door.

The undergrooms stayed by the stove, no fools they. In the dust-haunted depths, the horses moved, their breath steaming. "How many horses does his lordship keep?"

"Not so many as his father did," the man said. "Nor

so many as your father, miss. I mind well when every stall had a lovely face peering over the door."

"My father? Did you know him?"

He rubbed his hand over his short-cropped gray hair much as one would ruffle the fur of a dog. "Not to say 'knew,' ma'am, but I saw him often enough. A fine, fine figure of a man in the saddle, ma'am."

"Yes, he was. I shall tell my mother that you remember him."

"Do, ma'am. The name's Kellan. And here's your lovely mare, ma'am. Good shoulders she has, and such a pleasant disposition. Not like that de'il of yours, Your Grace."

"A devil to ride but a devil to go," Dominic said. "Have you been having much trouble with him? He should be tired enough to be docile."

"Not him, Your Grace. He'll be snapping at the Angel of Death, that one, and telling him to find another stallion to ride on his rounds."

"I hope so. Where is he?"

"There," Kellan pointed with his chin. "And your lady is next to him. They seem to get on."

"Do they indeed?" Sophie heard Dominic mutter.

Rosamund seemed content, certainly well cared for. Her mane was clear of tangles, her hooves shiny in the lantern light. She wore a brown plaid blanket while her breath steamed in the cold.

Sophie asked Dominic for some sugar. He came to her and put the pieces in her hand. Rosamund tossed up her head, demandingly. "Here then," Sophie said, holding out her hand. She felt the velvety nose nuzzling and marveled anew at the surprising delicacy of a huge animal's taking of a treat. An ill-tempered horse could bite off a finger in an instant, yet not one out of a thousand would do so.

"Aye, she's a proper highbred lady, she is," Kellan said, patting Rosamund's neck. "Would you have her papers, ma'am?"

"You'll have to ask his lordship. She's really his property."

"Ah. I must've misheard him, then." Kellan's gaze went past Sophie, his eyebrows rising.

Turning abruptly, Sophie caught Dominic with his hand in the air, evidently semaphoring some sort of message to the head groom. He transformed the gesture into a steadying pat on the top of his hat, turning on her a smile so innocent that any nanny worth her tatting would have suspected him at once of ill intentions.

Sophie only repeated, "She's his lordship's horse. Why? Were you thinking of having her covered?"

"That's right, ma'am. Good breeding always tells. Of course, His Grace would have to agree."

"You don't mean my horse, do you, Kellan?"

"Yes, Your Grace. Marry the power of one to the good manners of the other."

"It's a thought, Kellan, definitely a thought. Though his lordship prefers roses to horses."

"There's no accounting for tastes, Your Grace. Some men have an aversion to whiskey, which just leaves more for the rest of us, by my way of thinking."

"Good man," Dominic said, giving him a coin. "Every man needs a philosophy of life."

They couldn't leave without drinking a mug of tea, hot, stewed, and sweet. Though not to her taste, it had an undeniable warming effect. Between it and the odiferous stove, Sophie soon began to regret wearing her sister's fur-lined cloak.

The lads were shy of Sophie, being their mistress's sister and all, but Dominic soon had them at their ease. He had a knack for asking questions that elicited a person's most interesting tale about themselves or those they had known. Sophie saw that she wasn't the only person to find Dominic Swift remarkably easy to talk to.

When at last they could politely take their leave, Dominic had only walked a few feet away from the stable when he asked Sophie if she were cold.

"Not after that tea," she said, fanning herself with her hand.

"Would you care to walk about a little before we go inside?"

She remembered promising herself that she would avoid being alone with him. However, she should take advantage of the sunshine while it lasted, winter days were so brief. But she wouldn't allow herself to be drawn out again in that overflowing way. She had her pride to consider.

"Very well. Where shall we go?" Anywhere, she thought, but the rose garden. Seeing that place of rioting summer beauty shrouded and cold would be far too apt an analogy to her own life to be her choice.

"Why don't we walk toward the circular wood? It's prettier in the spring when the bluebells come out, but it should be peaceful now."

"Excellent. This way?"

"That's right. There's a sun dial in the middle of the wood. Silly place for it. The sun never strikes directly down among the trees except on noon on the solstice."

"I didn't know that, and I've lived in Finchley all my life."

"It must have been a pleasant place to grow up."

"It was," she said, following the path around a curve, "if you don't mind everyone knowing all about you. There are no secrets in a village, Your Grace. But tell me more about this wood. You said it was circular?"

"Ken's the one to tell you that tale. By daylight, if you are wise. He told me it late one night at school when we should have been asleep and it kept me awake for all of twenty minutes."

Her feet in their borrowed boots were growing cold, but she kept pace with him as best she could. "You were a sound sleeper as a child, I take it."

"I still am. It's quite all right, though. Fissing says a gentleman should never arise before eleven."

"I would have thought Fissing an early to bed, early to rise proponent."

"For himself, yes. For a gentlemen of leisure, perish the thought! Confidentially, however, I believe he likes me to lie abed so that I'm not in his way while he puts the house in order."

"I'm sure you're right," she said, a giggle escaping her.

"You should laugh more often," Dominic said.

She stopped, ignoring the snow that fell in the top of her boot. "If there's anything more calculated to stop a person laughing, it's saying something like that. Now, where's this circular wood?"

"At the top of this rise."

"And what's the tale about it?" she asked, gazing off into the distance. The path stopped about here.

"Several stories exist. Some say the Romans first planted the trees in imitation of their columned temples in Rome and sanctified it to the rites of Venus. Someone dug up a bronze cupid of about the right period not far from this spot a hundred years ago."

"Indeed. That makes it a reasonable explanation."

"Only the Romans weren't shy about building real temples when they wanted them. Another theory holds that this was a grove sacred to the Druids. Certainly the base of the present sundial is covered with faded marks that might be runes."

"I like that story. I think that's the one I'll believe."

"You're a romantic at heart, I think."

"Which story do you think is true?"

"The third one. I think Kenton's great-grandfather bought the base from a farmer who dug it up, planted a circular grove as an artistic conceit, and put a sundial in the middle because he was a cross-grained creature who lived for confusing his descendants."

Now Sophie did laugh out loud. He grinned at her like a fair magician who has turned an ordinary glass of water into three pigeons, an India-rubber ball, and a lit candle.

"Whether Roman temple, Druid shrine, or hoax, I'm not walking up there to see it today. My feet are cold and it must be time for luncheon."

"Agreed. Provided you'll walk up with me again at the solstice. Somehow I've never come here on that day, though I've often said I must."

"If I'm in Finchley then, I will, I promise."

"Half a promise. If. Terrible word."

"Very well, then," she said indulgently. "I promise."

"Good. And as a reward, you won't have to walk back to the house in wet—my goodness, they are wet, aren't they?"

Sophie hoped he wasn't planning to carry her. Just then, she heard the jingle of bells. Overtaking them quickly were several of the grooms from the stables, ropes over their shoulders, pulling along behind them a wooden sled with a rail around it and small bells dangling from the front.

"Here they are," Dominic said. "Madam, your chariot."

She couldn't refuse, not when the boys' tingling cheeks and bright eyes told her how fast they'd run.

With Dominic's help, she seated herself, arranging the cloak to hide her feet, tucking her hands inside her muff. "What about your luncheon?" she asked him.

"Tell them not to wait."

He nodded to the boys and they were running her away, their feet sinking into the snow but each urging the others on. Sophie looked back to see Dominic turn his face toward the circular grove on the hill and begin trudging toward it once more. She wondered which of the stories he'd told her was the one that drew him thither.

CHAPTER EIGHT

After dinner, Sophie indulged herself by playing the pianoforte. "I'm terribly stiff," she said when Dominic came over to turn the pages for her. "And out of practice," she added, hitting two wrong notes in a row.

"Are you a good pianist?" he asked.

"What, can't you hear that I have a rare gift?" she said, striking a flat instead of a sharp.

"I never studied music," he said. "But I do enjoy listening to other people play . . . well."

Sophie shook her head. "I hope to improve with application." She played a long arpeggio, nearly perfectly, then looked up at him, lifting her eyebrows, inviting comment.

"Not bad. You didn't play much in Italy, I take it?"

"Once in a while. Broderick played the flute and sometimes we'd meet with friends and hold a chamber evening. But Mr. Fulton, who played the cello, had to return to America, and took the piano with him."

"Speaking of Broderick," Dominic said, "how do you mean to organize his poems?"

"To be honest, I don't really know. I've been so distracted with this journey home. I have very little in mind beyond the mere determination to have them put before the public."

"I see."

"Do you have any suggestions?"

"Not at present. May I take them to read?"

"Certainly," she said, closing the piano lid. "I'll get them for you now."

"There's no hurry. I'll collect them before I go to bed." Dominic turned toward his friend, who was kicking idly at the fire.

"Is something wrong with Kenton?" Sophie whispered, under the pretext of cobbling together the music sheets.

"Looming fatherhood tends to sober a man, or so I've heard. I'd better talk to him."

Not wanting to have the appearance of an eavesdropper, Sophie drew her shawl more closely about her shoulders and went to the window. She drew back the curtain with one hand, looking out into the grounds. The silver candelabra on the rosewood piano cast a golden halo around her. Her reflection in the glass was ghostlike.

Outside, the snow seemed to have a light of its own, as does the moon. At first the woman who walked across the frozen crust appeared like a black shadow against the pale glow. Sophie couldn't even be sure there was someone there rather than an arrangement of shadows turned into human form by her own mind.

Sophie let the curtain fall behind her, cutting off the light. Now she could see far better. A woman indeed walked back and forth, a few yards at a time. Like Sophie, she wore only a shawl, insufficient against the cold.

Apparently someone else thought so, too. A streak of yellow light reached out across the snow from an opened door somewhere out of Sophie's sight. Another woman appeared—Lucia, the younger of the two Italian girls. The light showed up the spangles of melting ice in

Angelina's hair and the desperation of her face. She looked astonishingly beautiful but frightening as well, like a mask of tragedy.

Sophie couldn't hear what they said to each other. Obviously, Lucia urged her sister to come in out of the cold. Angelina shook her head so emphatically that some of her hair shook loose. Lucia gently tucked it behind her sister's ear and took her hand to lead her into the building. Angelina obviously didn't want to go, but slowly she began to walk along, her arms wrapped around her middle, Lucia's arm supporting her as if she were sick or wounded.

Sophie stepped back through the curtain. Dominic and Kenton were still in conference by the fireplace. She passed out of the room unnoticed, though when some instinct made her glance back, Dominic was smiling at her.

She hurried toward the servants' hall. Her mother, coming down the stairs, called to her. Sophie waited for her. "I think Angelina's ill, Mother. I was going to see."

"Dear me. I hope she hasn't brought anything contagious into this house."

"I doubt it. We were all given a clean bill of health when we arrived."

"Well, I shall go with you. If she's ill, she will have to see Dr. Richards at once. We mustn't risk any danger to Maris at this delicate time."

"No, of course not."

After a little effort, they found that the girls had gone to the room they shared on the third floor. Sophie persuaded her mother that it was unnecessary for her to climb the narrow steps that wound from the kitchens to the upper levels. She left her discussing the proper diet for a new mother with Mrs. Lemon.

Her candle threw weird shadows as Sophie climbed

up from one floor to the next. The Danesbys had not lavished so much attention on this part of the house, the carpet being of drugget and the banister a plain run of pine. Though the kitchen below was both warm and airy, the stairs were neither, being drafty and haunted by the smells of long-ago meals. She cupped her hand around the candle flame to keep it from blowing out. Sophie was relieved to see buckets of both water and sand on each landing in case of fire.

Emerging at last onto the third floor, Sophie looked for the fourth door on the right. This upper hall, though plainly papered and painted, had a welcoming look, if not temperature. A pretty blue vase stood upon a barley-twist table at the end of the narrow hall, adding a bit of color to a utilitarian area.

Even before Sophie found the door she sought, she heard the sound of idiomatic Italian spoken with great rapidity and a good deal of force. If there had been English people talking that quickly and with that volume, she would have broken in the door, anticipating a murder or at least a violent altercation. It had taken her several months of living in Rome to learn that when someone spoke very quickly and loudly, it didn't mean that they were angry with her.

She knocked and the voice, only one, stopped in mid word. After a moment, in which Sophie thought she heard whispering, someone said, "*Si?*"

"*Mi scusi, Lucia. Permesso?*"

"Ah, Signora Banner," Lucia said, opening the door a few inches. She wore a dressing gown, held tightly against her throat, her hair pouring like a waterfall over her shoulders. Her smile held no hint of anxiety, only sleepiness.

Sophie was surprised to see her ready for bed and said so. Lucia started on a long tale of having a

We'd Like to Invite You to Subscribe to Zebra's Regency Romance Book Club and Give You a Gift of 4 Free Books as Your Introduction! (Worth $19.96!)

If you're a Regency lover, imagine the joy of getting **4 FREE Zebra Regency Romances** and then the chance to have these lovely stories delivered to your home each month at the lowest price available! Well, that's our offer to you and here's how you benefit by becoming a Regency Romance subscriber:

* 4 FREE Introductory Regency Romances are delivered to your doorstep (you only pay for shipping and handling)

* 4 BRAND NEW Regencies are then delivered each month (usually before they're available in bookstores)

* Subscribers save almost $4.00 every month

* You also receive a FREE monthly newsletter, which features author profiles, discounts, subscriber benefits, book previews and more

* No risks or obligations...in other words, you can cancel whenever you wish with no questions asked

Join the thousands of readers who enjoy the savings and convenience offered to Regency Romance subscribers. After your initial introductory shipment, you receive 4 brand-new Zebra Regency Romances each month to examine for 10 days. Then, if you decide to keep the books, you'll pay the preferred subscriber's price, plus shipping and handling.

It's a no-lose proposition, so return the FREE BOOK CERTIFICATE today!

Say Yes to 4 Free Books!
Complete and return the order card to receive this $19.96 value, *ABSOLUTELY FREE!*

If the certificate is missing below, write to:
Regency Romance Book Club
P.O. Box 5214, Clifton, New Jersey 07015-5214
or call TOLL-FREE 1-800-770-1963
Visit our website at www.kensingtonbooks.com.

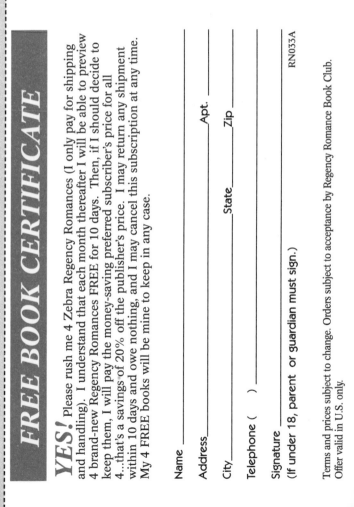

FREE BOOK CERTIFICATE

YES! Please rush me 4 Zebra Regency Romances (I only pay for shipping and handling). I understand that each month thereafter I will be able to preview 4 brand-new Regency Romances FREE for 10 days. Then, if I should decide to keep them, I will pay the money-saving preferred subscriber's price for all 4...that's a savings of 20% off the publisher's price. I may return any shipment within 10 days and owe nothing, and I may cancel this subscription at any time. My 4 FREE books will be mine to keep in any case.

Name _____

Address _____ Apt. _____

City _____ State_____ Zip _____

Telephone ( ) _____

Signature _____
(If under 18, parent or guardian must sign.)   RN033A

Terms and prices subject to change. Orders subject to acceptance by Regency Romance Book Club.
Offer valid in U.S. only.

A
$19.96
VALUE...
FREE!

No
obligation
to buy
anything,
ever!

‖‖..ı..ıı‖ı.....ıı.ı.ıı.ı.ı.ıı.ıı.ı.ıı..ı.ıı..ıı.ıı..ı

REGENCY ROMANCE BOOK CLUB
Zebra Home Subscription Service, Inc.
P.O. Box 5214
Clifton NJ 07015-5214

PLACE
STAMP
HERE

headache and wishing to go to sleep early. Not being able to ask for permission from the upper servants and not wishing to disturb Sophie, she'd retired on her own responsibility. "*Ma, Angelina aiuterà, signora.*"

"*Non è importante, grazie.*"

But Lucia insisted it was important and that Angelina would be down to wait on Signora Banner in not more than half an hour. A voice from within the room made Lucia turn her head to listen. She said something short and sharp which, nonetheless, made Angelina laugh. Sophie heard something about a barking dog, one of those Italian phrases for which she'd never understood the meaning behind the words.

Sophie wished Lucia a good evening and a restful night. Somewhat puzzled, she picked up her candle from the hall table and descended the narrow back staircase. Perhaps she'd misinterpreted what she'd seen outside. Angelina no longer seemed to be in emotional distress. People were incalculable. Angelina had not seemed like a volatile personality, either in Rome or on the ship. Therefore, if she were laughing now, she probably hadn't been overset outside.

Mrs. Lindel having left the kitchen, Sophie went in search of her to reassure her that she had nothing to worry about. No one was ill. There would be no risk to Maris or her child.

Mrs. Lindel had returned to the drawing room. Sophie entered, looking about her. "Where are the men?"

"They've gone to play billiards and probably to smoke, if I know men. How is your little maid?"

"Perfectly well. I don't know what made me think she was ill."

"I do so hope you're not going to become prophetic, dearest. I had a great-aunt who used to see visions of great events before they happened."

"Did you? I never heard this tale," Sophie said, sinking down on an ottoman at her mother's feet.

Mrs. Lindel laid the *Ladies' Magazine* down on her knee, marking her place with her finger. "Oh, yes. My mother's aunt used to see the most terrible visions at the most inconvenient times. One would be entertaining the bishop or some such person when Great-Aunt Oralie would shout out some nonsense about flying chariots or black clouds of doom hovering over people."

"How embarrassing."

"To say the least."

"Why did she do it?"

"Who can say? I was so young all I could do was cringe. Now that I'm older, I believe I understand. I think it was a desire to improve a rather dull existence by making herself interesting. She never married nor, I believe, did anyone ever wish to marry her. With so little to think about, who can blame her for inventing a talent for prophecy?"

"No, I couldn't blame her. If anything, I envy her," Sophie said, staring down at the pale gold glint of her wedding band.

"Envy her?"

"I wish my life had been that dull. I would rather have imaginary troubles."

"And no love?" Her mother's eyes were kind and wise, deep wells of both love and sorrow.

"I was happy when I thought Broderick loved me. Perhaps he even did, for a little while."

"Did you love him longer than a little while?"

"Yes, for all the good it did me."

"I'm not sure that doing oneself good is the reason we seek after love. Tell me. Do you blame me for not stopping you as I could have done?"

Sophie glanced up and surprised a tear on her

mother's face. Instantly she reached up to clasp her hand. "No. I never thought that for one instant. Marrying him was my choice. When it went wrong, that was my fault as much as his."

"He misled you about the life he saw for the two of you."

"No, I think I misled myself. I can't be sure at this point what Broderick wanted. I only know it wasn't what I had to offer."

Mrs. Lindel patted Sophie's cheek with her petal-soft fingers. "I didn't realize Broderick was so blind. How any man, looking at you, could look elsewhere . . ."

"Ah, but you didn't see Catherine Margrave. An olive-skinned, plump brunette with cupid's-bow lips and the most enchanting beauty spot above her left cheekbone. She had strange, light green eyes, in piquant contrast to her coloring. All the men were mad for her at first sight."

"You knew her, then?"

"Certainly," Sophie said lightly, sitting back on her heels. "We met some weeks before Broderick ever saw her. I actually liked her very much."

"Then she betrayed you when she stole your husband."

"Broderick was very attractive. And . . ." she hesitated, cobbling together her thought and philosophy. "I don't believe that anyone can steal another's love. She didn't hit Broderick on the head and drag him off to live with her. He went most willingly, even joyfully."

"It's hard for me to understand such a man. Your father never would have made that sort of break with me, however many mistresses he had in keeping."

"Mother? He didn't . . ."

"I don't know. I suspected sometimes, but we never spoke of it and actually, now that I look back, I can't be sure. No one who mattered, at any rate."

Sophie could see herself being willfully blind about such matters if Broderick had only let that be an option. "When I look at your marriage and Maris's, it does give me hope that mine was no more than an aberration."

The ormolu clock above the marble fireplace chimed with crystal clarity. "Is it so late? We'd better retire if we are to visit Miss Bowles early."

"True." Sophie leaned on her mother's chair and stood up. "I think I'll find a book and read for a little first. I've had so little time to read lately."

"I'll go look in on Maris. Kenton said she was very tired tonight."

Sophie paused mid step. "Do you think it will be soon?"

"Before Christmas, I think. Her silhouette has changed."

"Oh. Oh, I see, I think." Sophie leashed her thoughts, not wanting to travel down that path. Though she had once believed herself pregnant for several weeks the summer after she was married, she had never imagined the details of childbirth. Though her disappointment had been intense at the time, she'd soon realized it was all for the best. Now she was torn between excitement at the birth of her niece or nephew and sympathy for what Maris would soon suffer.

A book had suddenly become a necessity. She took up one of the chambersticks waiting for the household at the bottom of the stairs. Dimly, she heard the men laughing in the room sacred to sport. It sounded as though Dominic has succeeded in raising Kenton's spirits. She felt an impulse to go in there, to spend a few minutes in cheerful company. Women, her beloved family, seemed to want to turn her over and shake out all the loose bits, as if she were a broken clock. Dominic—that is to say, men—didn't do that. They were content to talk about impersonal matters.

She walked toward the sound of their voices. Before she'd gone very far, however, she thought the better of it. No doubt they had their coats off, their cravats undone. She would only disturb their comfort.

She turned back. Book, then bed. In the morning, she'd have the exhausting duty of consulting about dress. Sophie wished she could pretend to be a mere doll, a female-shaped object to be dressed as wiser heads decreed. Knowing herself, however, she foresaw that she'd struggle fruitlessly against her mother and sister's advice.

The library fire had died down to a mere glow. Which explained perhaps why Sophie shivered when she walked into the room. Her candle flickered, casting shadows that raced over the walls in a *danse macabre*. Cupping her hand about it, she stepped to the bookcases. Somewhere there must be a book that would calm her thoughts.

A rustle registered only as a sound to be expected in a library, the sound of paper or curtain. Yet an instinct deeper than civilization allowed spoke. Sophie felt her whole body tighten. With utter care, she turned her head.

The dark was cave-like. Her single flame penetrated only a few feet and had the sole effect of making the darkness darker yet. Sophie suddenly realized that having the only light was not a good thing at all. She couldn't see, but stood exposed to the hostile eyes she instinctively knew were focused upon her.

"Sophie?"

When a deep voice spoke her name, a strangled scream broke from her lips and her hand flew up. The candle dropped, snuffing itself on the carpet. "Dominic," she whispered hoarsely. "Someone's here."

A swirling blast of frigid air tore through the room, driving spicules of ice against her skin. The French door at the far end of the room slammed, breaking a pane of glass.

Dominic ran past her, touching her back fleetingly, and pursued. Sophie fell back to the doorway and shouted for help and light. As if echoing her demand, she heard a dog barking wildly somewhere beyond the walls of the house.

She had no notion that Finchley held so many souls. People seemed to pour out like ants when their nest is stirred by a stick. Half a dozen maidservants appeared, including Lucia and Angelina, some screaming before even knowing what was happening. Boots and footmen came storming from behind the green baize door, youngest and oldest alike dancing with excitement and alarm. The haughty month-nurse who kept strictly to herself in the empty nursery ran down the stairs and added to the confusion by tripping on the first step and riding down the rest on her tailbone.

When Tremlow appeared, stately as a great galleon scattering lesser vessels in the way, the cacophony died away to near quiet, punctuated only by the whimpering of the poor month-nurse.

Sophie grabbed Kenton's arm. "He's gone out after him."

"Who?"

"Dominic. There was someone in the library. He frightened me. Dominic ran after him."

"Who was it?"

"I don't know. It was dark." She drew in a shaky breath. "I went in for a book. There was someone there."

"All right," he said. "Men, search the grounds. Tremlow, send someone to alert the stables."

"Very good, my lord." He pointed two lordly fingers at the boots. "The stables, at once."

"Yes, Mr. Tremlow."

Kenton seized a branched candelabra from the cook's trembling hands and led the way into the library. "Throw some logs on the fire, someone."

"Sophie, what's toward?" her mother asked, making her way through the milling servants. Her gray hair lay in waves on her shoulders, her wrapper caught to her bosom with one hand. "Are you all right?" she demanded, putting her arm about Sophie's shoulders.

The sight of her mother's concerned frown made Sophie pull herself together. "I came in for a book and I surprised an intruder. That's all. He ran away as soon as Dominic appeared."

"You're not hurt? He didn't touch you?"

"No, I'm fine." She smiled at her mother with a courage that ceased to be feigned after a moment or so.

Kenton was by now examining the broken window, stepping gingerly amid the pieces of glass, some crushed to powder by Dominic's racing feet. Sophie came closer, stopping on the end of the carpet, where the glass and the blowing snow hadn't reached.

"That happened when the burglar ran out."

Kenton steadied the door, which had a tendency to swing in the icy breeze. He frowned at the white woodwork. "I think . . ." he began to say.

Mrs. Lemon lifted a wavering hand, pointing over Kenton's head. "Look, look there."

A man appeared, wraithlike on the other side of the windows. Everyone stared, even the master of the house. Then Dominic pushed against Kenton's hold. "Let a fellow in. I'm colder than a fish."

"What happened?" Ken demanded, throwing open the door. Dominic and Tip entered, spattered with snow.

Sophie looked around and saw the figured silk-and-wool shawl Maris had been wearing earlier in the evening thrown over the back of a settee. She took it up, feeling the weight and warmth with pleasure. Without saying a word, she reached up on her toes to drape the shawl around Dominic's shoulders. The fabric of his coat showed darker spots where the snow had melted. His hair, too, had turned darker, especially where he raked it back from his forehead. He grasped the shawl and threw her an absent smile before his attention was once more captured by what Kenton was showing him.

"There's blood here," he said.

That was too much for the cook. She gave a piercing scream, startling every one, and tottered, first one way and then another. Though far from the overly plump cook of common knowledge, she nonetheless knocked down the tweeny and Lucia when she collapsed.

Dominic met Sophie's eyes and his lips twitched uncontrollably. She felt the laughter rising up like champagne inside a shaken bottle. A few giggles escaped and she coughed to disguise it, lest someone assume she was hysterical.

"It's not my blood," Dominic said, holding up his hands one after the other to show that there were no wounds anywhere.

Poor Mrs. Lemon had roused just enough to hear the word "blood" again and promptly crashed down. This time the tweeny managed to sidestep her and avoid being flattened.

"Therefore, it seems as if we must look for someone with a cut on their hand," Kenton said, turning his head briefly at the noise of the fall. "I've sent the men out to search."

"They won't find anything. I was following the footprints, but the snow is blowing around and wiping them out."

Sophie spoke up. "Let's discuss this elsewhere before Dominic—and poor Tip—catch their death."

They all looked down at the dog. He looked up, his sherry-colored eyes alert. A rag hung from the corner of his mouth. "What's that?" Kenton said, bending low. "Come on, boy. Give it up."

He held it out on his palm. An irregularly torn piece of fabric, two inches square, of some rough material, it had evidently been ripped from some larger piece. "Our poor burglar is an unlucky devil. First he cuts his hand, then Tip gets a hold on his best trousering."

"You'd better keep it. That's a valuable piece of evidence," Dominic said, shivering.

"You go change your clothes and dry your hair," Sophie demanded. "I'll make tea, as Mrs. Lemon is indisposed."

He snapped to attention, saluting sharply. "You have but to command, ma'am."

CHAPTER NINE

"It seems I missed all the excitement," Maris complained, waiting for the carriage the next morning. "I cannot believe that no one bothered to awaken me, not even Kenton."

"Did you scold him for it?" Sophie asked.

"Indeed. I hold that a man has certain responsibilities toward his wife, one of which is certainly to awaken her when the house is under siege by bandits."

"Just one bandit," Sophie said, "And he, it seems, didn't steal anything."

"Now that's very curious. As almost everything at Finchley is an heirloom, I may as well admit that we have a plethora of beautiful things. Quite a lot of it is portable, as well."

"Yet he stole nothing. That is odd."

"I can only assume that you interrupted this burglar before he could carry out whatever plans he had." Maris patted Sophie's hand. "I'm very grateful to you and Dominic. Did he really chase after him into the dark? And on such a bitter night?"

"He did indeed. Without an instant's hesitation."

At the time, she had not thought very much about his courage in running out into the dark. Anything might have been waiting for him, from a shot to a club on the head. Yet he hadn't hesitated. She could still feel the touch of his hand as he went past her.

"Are you all right?" Maris asked.

"Very well, thank you."

"You shivered."

"Did I? There must be a draft."

Maris looked around the entryway. "I suppose so." Distracted by the arrival of the carriage, she took her sister's arm. "Where's Mother? Go see if you can find her. Kenton doesn't like it when we keep the horses standing in the cold."

"Certainly." Throwing open her pelisse, Sophie went in search of her mother.

She found her talking to Kenton and Dominic in the library. "Mother? The carriage is here."

"Is it? Excellent, we'll go at once. I can't wait until you are dressed as you should be. Don't you think so, gentlemen?"

What could they do but agree? Sophie looked at them with an understanding smile. Kenton agreed instantly, siding with his mother-in-law—no fool he.

Dominic cleared his throat. "I see no fault in Mrs. Banner's appearance as she stands."

Sophie didn't mind that he said it; it was good to hear that she didn't offend *everybody's* eyes. However, she could have wished he hadn't declared his admiration quite so publicly. Her mother was already wearing the same speculative expression Sophie had seen on Maris's face.

"Is it true . . . Maris told me that nothing was stolen last night."

"Nothing we've been able to discover. Tremlow and the others have been taking a painstaking inventory. Tremlow knows every piece of plate, every picture, every objet d'art better than I do myself, and I own them. If our thief had made off with so much as a thimble, Tremlow would know."

"Then did I simply interrupt before he could do whatever he came for? Maris thinks that is what happened."

"I think so, too."

Dominic reached out to touch her lightly on the wrist. "Don't do that again."

"I didn't mean to do it the first time." She turned to her mother. "We mustn't keep the horses standing. And Miss Bowles will be waiting."

The snow muffled the sound of the horses' hooves and the wheels so that it seemed as if the carriage was flying silently through the air. Everything she saw was black, gray, or white. The dark trees drooped with the weight of the snowfall like old men carrying too many heavy sacks. A few ravens flapped into the steel-colored sky with halfhearted calls.

The view was no brighter in the village, except where the red clay soil was exposed at the edge of the road. The half-timbered front of the inn and the gray bulk of the church, at opposite ends of the spectrum socially, made a pleasing, if somber, composition. Miss Bowles's little house, clinging to the far end of the village, came as a bit of a shock to an eye grown accustomed to the monochromatic landscape. While no more than a house of dirty white brick, some unskilled hand had painted the shutters and front door a lively shade of crimson. A streak, fading now, even decorated the doorstep.

Sophie glanced with raised eyebrows at her family. Maris eased her position in the corner. "I can't remember if you have ever met Miss Bowles."

"No, she moved here after Sophie went to Rome. She's daughter of Miss Menthrip's cousin. She came to look after Miss Menthrip."

"Then why does she live here? Miss Menthrip lives down at the other end."

Mrs. Lindel's smile, had it been less good-natured, would have qualified as a smirk. "I'm afraid Miss Menthrip didn't appreciate Miss Bowles as much as she might have done."

"Miss Menthrip isn't exactly simplicity itself to live with, either," Maris said tartly. She had lived with Miss Menthrip for some weeks before Kenton had proposed and was one of the few people of whom Miss Menthrip spoke with favor. "Miss Bowles had a difficult time adjusting to her sharp tongue. I could never persuade her that Miss Menthrip did not mean all that she said."

The crimson door opened and a woman peered out. She wore her dark hair very high, almost high enough for a formal ball. The face under the creation, however, was meek and unassuming, with slightly protuberant eyes and a bumpy chin inexpertly covered with powder. But her smile, when she realized her customers had arrived, was truly beautiful, for she had better teeth and a more generous mouth than either Maris or Sophie.

Despite the cold, she stepped into the street. Sophie emerged from the carriage. "Good morning," she said, holding out her hand to greet little Miss Bowles. "It's a great pleasure to meet you."

"Oh, it's my honor, ma'am. If you knew how I've longed to see Italy . . . you must forgive me if I pester you with questions."

"Ask what you like," Sophie said, unable to remember when she'd ever taken a greater liking to someone at first sight. "If I can answer, I will."

"Oh, thank you. Here's her ladyship! I never thought she'd come, in her condition," she added, dropping her voice. "I shall run in and put another cushion in her chair." Good as her word, she whisked inside as the footman assisted Lady Danesby to descend.

The plume on her hat tossed and bounced as she awkwardly sought with her foot for the step she could not see. The young man looked terrified of dropping his mistress. His arms shook with strain as he reached up for her hand and elbow.

Sophie wanted to put her hand up to cover her eyes, her mind's eye putting up a detailed image of Maris tumbling to the ground. Then Maris had successfully negotiated the step and stood beside her sister. "There," she said.

"Maris, my love, please don't do that again," Sophie said.

"What?"

"Come out. If Kenton saw you, he'd collapse or forbid you to leave the house. It's wrong to risk everything like this."

Sophie wouldn't have blamed Maris if she'd been angry. Though their mother had asked her to intervene, Sophie knew it wasn't her place to criticize or comment on Maris's choices. After all, most of Maris's decisions had been successful. She had a husband who adored her, a baby on the way, and a position in society that would never diminish.

Maris drew Sophie aside. "Mother suggested you tell me that, didn't she?"

"I was going to say it even if she hadn't. I don't have any idea about what it is like to be in your condition, but don't you think it would be wise to rest more?"

"I can't. I'm so restless now. If I had to stay cooped up at home, I think I should run mad. With nothing to do but brood on what may so easily go amiss . . . no. Better to shock the neighbors than to let my thoughts swirl around this one idea."

"What idea?"

She rolled her tear-filled eyes toward the sky, wiping away the moisture that threatened to roll down her face. "The notion that everything will go disastrously wrong. That I, or worse still, my child, will die."

"No," Sophie declared immediately.

"It may happen. It happened to Princess Charlotte and it happens to countless others every day. I cannot believe myself so blessed that I can escape this doom."

"But if you don't rest, you may be ensuring such a result. Listen, I will do whatever you want. Shall I read to you by the hour or regale you with stories of life in Rome? I saw the Pope once. I could spend several hours describing every detail if you would find it entertaining."

Maris gave a laugh that was almost a sob. "I suppose I might stay home under those circumstances."

"And I can't speak for His Grace, but can you doubt that Kenton would devote himself to your entertainment?"

"Devoting himself thus is how I wound up in this condition," Maris said ruefully. She swiftly pressed her fingers to her lips, her eyes laughing over the nails. "I must guard my tongue. Miss Bowles would be shocked beyond all bounds."

"As I myself," Sophie said with mock severity. "Remember my widowed state."

Maris caught her by the sleeve. "Mother's waiting. But tell me—do you miss that part of marriage? I do."

"I miss the way I felt in the beginning. That racing in the blood, that carelessness . . . I don't believe it lasts."

Maris smiled at her. "It lasts. Believe me."

"Girls," their mother called, much as she used to when they were young and heedless. "Girls, let's go inside."

The carriage drove off, turning around so that man

and beast alike could find refreshment and shelter at the King's Oak. The women went into Miss Bowles's house, the front room of which served as her studio and workroom.

Sophie paid no attention to the greetings between the others, drawn as though by unearthly power to the fabrics in the corner of the room, where what dim sun there was could fall upon them. The colors glowed as if with their own light. Here were the shades her mother and sister had described to her, pale gray, a color insubstantial as smoke, and yet another with the mixing shades of a gray pearl laid over with tones of lavender. Lilac and rich purple shone like flowers in spring, with the crisp contrast of white lace foaming over the edge of the bolt. There was also linen, white and fresh, to make new tuckers, caps, and nightgear. The ribbons were in keeping with the discreet colors of half mourning, that neither-flesh-nor-fowl stage a widow entered upon after six months. Still and all, the luxuriousness of these fabrics more than compensated for any lack of brilliance. She'd never been one to dress outlandishly; even her bride clothes had been chosen more for practicality than beauty.

She turned to her mother and gave her a kiss on the cheek and a hug about the waist. "I'm in your hands, entirely and without reservation. Choose what you think is best for me and I shan't say a word against it."

Naturally, once they began pulling out the books and planning what appearance each creation was to take, Sophie could not keep silent. Mrs. Lindel merely smiled and left it to Maris, adding her own suggestions from an easy chair, to remind Sophie of her promise.

"Very well," Mrs. Lindel said at the end of an exhaustive discussion. "Which shall we have first?"

Miss Bowles considered. "The gray poplin could be

made up in four days, if I could hire the Granger girls from the King's Oak to help."

The gray poplin was as close to blue as might be seemly. The sleeves were to be long and full, with a fascinating frill at the wrist to show off her hands. Three lines of narrow tucking around the hem would draw attention to her small feet. Sophie found herself wondering what appearance she would present in such a confection. If someone thought her handsome in her present attire, what light of admiration might be kindled in a pair of blue eyes when she wore such a gown?

She could not fool herself. She knew she was thinking of Dominic. Though she had determined never to marry again, she still retained enough girlishness to wish to see flattering approval in the eyes of a man. Sophie vowed to exterminate this wish in herself lest she turn into an arrant flirt.

Maris spoke up from her corner, where she held a magazine open upon her lap. "I am of the opinion that the first gown to be sewn should be this ball dress made from the heavy pearl gray satin."

"Ball dress?" Sophie exclaimed. "I don't need one, do I?"

"Oh, that's right," Mrs. Lindel said. "Miss Bowles, you can hire whom you please. My daughter must have a suitable gown by the twenty-fourth."

"Yes, indeed," the spinster said, tapping her fingers against her cheek. "Very wise of you, your ladyship. I shall start at once. I have only to finish the hem of Mrs. Ward's dress, but one of the Granger girls can easily do that. Let me just confirm these measurements."

While Miss Bowles scurried around Sophie with her measure, Maris gave her reasons. "Have you forgotten about Reginald Lively's Christmas fete?"

"He stopped giving it when his wife passed away."

"He started up again last year," Mrs. Lindel said. "It's quieter than it used to be, not quite such a bacchanalia, if you can use such a term for a country Christmas. All the same, there will be dancing, amateur theatricals, and a feast. Maris is right; you must have a proper gown."

"I only wish I could go with Kenton. You would not credit how beautifully he dances," Maris said. "But I have every confidence that Dominic will most willingly be your seigneur for the ball." She paused, then added slyly, "If you agree, Mother."

"Who could ask for a more gallant cavalier?" Mrs. Lindel said rhetorically, while Miss Bowles giggled and Sophie looked askance at them all.

After visiting Mrs. Ward and her husband at the rectory, they had planned to visit Miss Menthrip in company. But Maris proclaimed that she was tired and wished to go home to put her feet up. Sophie, who liked Miss Menthrip very much, ran across the street, but found the acid-tongued spinster from home. She slipped one of Mrs. Lindel's visiting cards under the door and hurried back. The carriage was already waiting at the vicarage door.

Dominic heard the ladies return, their chatter and laughter at the door bringing life back into the house. He'd stayed here often during Kenton's bachelor days. Though the decor and efficiency of the household had not changed, there was a new spirit here, directly attributable to the Lindel women. He felt it more strongly yet now that Sophie had come to stay. He knew he'd realize the lack of it all the more when he had to leave.

She came in, smoothing her hair upward where it had been disarranged by her bonnet. Her smile, when she saw him, held so much friendly warmth that he involuntarily looked behind him to see whom she might be smiling at.

"Did you have good hunting?" he asked.

"Very good indeed. This time next week, you won't know me."

"Then I shall have the pleasure of meeting you all over again."

"Oh, have you been reading them?" she asked, nodding toward the lion's-mask box, open before where he'd been sitting.

"The poems? Yes, I began a little while ago. He was remarkably inventive, this poet of yours." Saying that was rather like testing a sore tooth with one's tongue. The twinge was exquisitely painful, yet not enough to make one stop doing it as would be the sensible thing to do.

"Yes, he was very clever. Yet there is feeling there as well, don't you find?"

"You've read them all, I suppose," he asked, evading the question.

"Most of them. I'm afraid I rather avoided reading some of the ones addressed to Catherine Margrave."

"His—I beg your pardon, Sophie. I mean, Mrs. Banner."

"You might as well call me by my name. I've been thinking of you as Dominic ever since Dover."

"Have you?"

She nodded blithely. "I saw you from the ship and I thought, 'Oh, look. There's Dominic. What's he doing here?' and I haven't been able to think of you as 'Your Grace' since."

"You've called me that, though. I didn't like it. You should call me Dominic. Always."

She turned to the poems again, and he realized he'd gone too far, too fast. When would he learn not to be greedy? He learned as a child not to ask for the impossible, but had forgotten his lesson some time after gaining all those things which the world deemed important. He foresaw that Sophie would teach him many lessons.

"Yes," she said in answer to his unasked question. "Catherine Margrave was his mistress. Where she's gone to, I don't know. I'd heard a rumor that as soon as Broderick died, she went to Austria. There was a Viennese count, I think it was, who'd tried to lure her away from Broderick. I will say this much for her, she was loyal. Broderick had no money, no position, nothing but genius. I believe she would have stayed with him forever, if he hadn't died."

Dominic couldn't understand it. That runty, vainglorious poet with the calculating eye had persuaded two women to fall desperately in love with him, and he couldn't even manage one. It was enough to make a man become a poet, one of the bitterly vituperative variety.

"Was he living with you at the time of his death or with this other woman?" Dominic asked. "I don't mean to give you pain. If it's none of my business, just say so."

"I don't mind," she said, sitting down at the writing desk. She looked at the open box of papers warily, as if it contained some animal that might bite. "He left me to live with La Margrave six months or so before he died. Actually, though, he perished while on a walking tour of Sicily with Mr. Knox, whom you met."

"How did he come to die? He seemed in good health."

"Any man might fall, and he did. Mr. Knox found his body and had him buried there in Sicily. He wasn't Catholic, but there's a cemetery in Palermo for foreigners."

He offered her no condolences, which relieved her mind. She was tired of explaining the whys and wherefores of her unhappy marriage. Broderick had abandoned her. He died. Now there was only this last duty, the one thing she felt she must finish before looking ahead to any kind of new life.

Reaching out, she pulled a poem from the box. It wasn't one she recognized, and she knew all the ones he'd written while they were together. It seemed to be about prayer, though knowing Broderick, it was probably about his mistress or a particularly good dinner he'd eaten as an undergraduate. One was just as likely as another at first glance. It was only after study and analyzation that one came to understand the subtle play of his language and the depth of his gifts.

She laid down "Dawn in the Piazza San Pietro" and looked across at Dominic. He had leaned his head on his hand, his fingers moving idly through his thick hair. She didn't need to see his face to know that he was frowning intently. She waited for him to understand what he read.

The moment was not long in coming. He looked up, as startled as someone who is suddenly called. "This is you," he said. "You are here in every line. When did he write this?"

She took the poem from his hand. "'Epithalamium,'" she read. "Yes, he wrote this shortly after we were married. I suppose I really was 'like the petal of a flower not yet open.'"

"Yes, you were."

Her smile was intentionally teasing. "A gallant gentleman would say that I still am."

"No. You're open now."

"To say the least." She chuckled softly. "Open but not yet fallen, I hope."

CHAPTER TEN

Dominic grew so involved in the poems that midnight struck without his hearing it. Then he came upon one addressed to "Catherine, My Fair" and pushed the whole box away with such a sharp gesture that it fell over.

He now felt that he knew Broderick Banner very well. So much genius allied with so little self-confidence was outside his experience. When he made his living with his pen, he'd met many a brilliant fellow who swaggered and the number of fools who were ashamed of themselves were far outnumbered by those proud of their ignorance. Perhaps some of the more egregious boasters had been hiding a deep sense of self-doubt under their self-aggrandizement.

Yet whenever he started to feel sorry for Broderick, he would think of the new hardness in Sophie's eyes, and his pity would blow aside like dust. He wished now that he'd risked more that night when he'd asked her to run away with him. If only he'd been able to persuade her, how much unhappiness would she have missed. All his vaunted gifts with words had proved useless when it came to gaining the one woman he'd wanted.

Unable to sit still another moment, Dominic jumped up and began pacing back and forth. The friendship he'd begun to create with Sophie had real satisfactions. Working together, even on her late husband's poems, would bring them closer still. But he had to be careful not to want more, not even in his deepest heart. To want more would be the surest way never to have more. "My God," he said aloud, "how I hate paradox."

He was brought out of his reverie by a clatter from the hall. The thudding of a pair of booted feet running down the staircase, sliding, nearly falling, sent Dominic to the door. Kenton was facing him yet ran into him anyway, as if he were blind. Dominic caught him by the elbows and fended him off. "What is it? Maris?"

"Yes, just now." He wore only a shirt, breeches, and his boots. "She woke me."

"Did you tell her mother?"

"No. I have to go for the doctor." He struggled to get free from Dominic's gentle grasp.

"You wake Mrs. Lindel. She'll know what to do for Maris. *I'll* go fetch the doctor."

"You will?" Kenton patted him on the shoulders with both hands. "Yes. You go. Hurry," he said, steering Dominic toward the front door. "There should be a horse saddled. I gave orders that one should always be ready, just in case."

"Good thinking," Dominic said, digging in his heels lest he be propelled bodily through the closed door. "Let me get my coat, there's a good fellow." He disengaged from Kenton, not without difficulty, and stepped back into the library to yank the bellpull.

Tremlow appeared as silently as a spirit materialization. Though wearing a scarlet dressing gown instead of his usual neat attire, his sangfroid suffered not a jot from being summoned in the middle of the night.

"My coat and hat, Tremlow," Dominic said. "I'm riding for the doctor's house. Can you tell me where it is?"

"I can tell you," Kenton said. "It's perfectly simple."

He opened his mouth, hesitated, and turned to the butler. "Where the devil *does* he live?"

Being cut from the same cloth as Fissing, Tremlow showed his emotions only by the slightest widening of his eyes. "Take the main road to the village, Your Grace, taking the first turning just shy of the church. Dr. Richards resides behind the third door of the block of attached dwellings on your left. You'll have to knock vigorously; his domestics are notoriously heavy sleepers."

"Thank you, Tremlow. You'd best pour out some brandy for his lordship."

"No," Kenton said. "I can't go to Maris with alcohol on my breath. Coffee, Tremlow. Pots of it."

"Very good, my lord. Godspeed, Your Grace."

Even with the thick woolen muffler that Tremlow added to his attire, Dominic felt that there were minuscule knives striking his face as he rode. Blinking hard, he put his head down and encouraged his stallion onward. Phrenicos showed a marked disinclination to head straight into the wind-driven ice droplets. But Dominic was afraid that if once the horse left the road, thickly coated though it was, they'd flounder in the ditch.

"Come on, my lad, come on," he murmured. "I don't blame you, 'deed I don't, but there's a charming lady who needs us."

Dominic felt the horse gather himself beneath him, as if he understood. With a greater energy, they passed through the trees and up the slight rise in the road. The wind seemed straight from Greenland as they came into the open, but Phrenicos had the pace now and continued on.

Dismounting after following Tremlow's directions, which were as excellent as might be expected, Dominic passed the reins under his arm and took the horse right up the steps. Recollecting Tremlow's advice, Dominic pounded on the door like a battering ram.

A window opened above his head with a screech of wet wood. "What is it? Who's there? Good Gad, is that a horse? I'm not dosing a horse, not again."

Dominic stepped back, seeking the source of the voice. "Dr. Richards?"

"If I'm not, young man, you've woken me up for nothing. What's amiss?"

"Lady Danesby. She's . . . well . . ."

"Now? She's a week ahead. Ah, well, it's a rare baby that comes on schedule. You're not Sir Kenton?" the doctor asked, peering down.

"No. I'm a friend. I didn't want Kenton to ride so far."

"Nervous, is he?"

"One could say that."

"Go back. Tell them I'll be there as soon as I harness the horse."

"May I do that for you?"

"No, I thank you. My man eats his head off all day. I don't mind waking him up even if I have to use a cold sponge."

Phrenicos traveled more willingly with the wind behind him and a comfortable stable ahead. The head groom received him with the sort of pride one usually found in a father. He motioned Dominic out of the saddle at almost the same instant he rode into the yard.

Sophie stood at the rear door, a lamp held low. "Dominic?"

"The doctor will be here as soon as he can." He took off his coat and low-crowned hat as he stepped in, knocking quite a lot of ice on the floor. Sophie all but leaped out of the way with a very out-of-character squeak.

He glanced down and paused in the act of unknotting the scarf from around his throat. Her feet were bare—

pale, arched, with the loveliest, straightest toes he'd ever seen. The instant she realized he was looking, she sank down a little so her dressing gown covered her feet. "I can't find my slippers," she said defiantly. "I think I left them in Rome."

"I see."

"I'm certainly not going to trouble my mother for a pair, not right now."

"Don't your feet get cold?"

"Not until someone drops snow all over the floor." She tried to sound stern, but her pink cheeks gave away her true feelings.

"Why didn't you just put on a pair of shoes?" he asked.

Her brows drew together and she sought for words. "I didn't think of it. I must be more excited than I realized. I'd better go tell Kenton that the doctor is on the way."

"How is he holding up?"

"I don't know. He hasn't left her side."

He walked with her to the stair, wishing he dared pick her up and keep her feet from the cold floor. The only reason he didn't do it is that he wanted her to talk to him again in his lifetime.

Sophie started up the steps, then stopped, half turning to look down at him. Her double-breasted wrapper twisted at the waist, accentuating her slenderness. "There's coffee in the morning room if you want to warm up. Will you stay awake or go to bed?"

"I think I'll stay up. It's not every day a fellow becomes a godfather."

"You?" Her smile warmed his heart more than any coffee ever brewed. "Then we have something in common. I'm also a godparent, as well as an aunt."

"There you have me. I can't very well be an uncle, too, not without . . ." Dominic realized a moment too late where this piece of humor was leading. His guilty expression summoned a blush into her cheeks.

"I'll just . . ." she said, pointing awkwardly behind herself. "I'll just . . ." She hurried up the stairs.

When she came down again, she had put on a round gown and a pair of shoes.

Dominic, calling himself every kind of fool, set himself the task of making her quite easy and comfortable again. The circumstances of their being awake so late, however, kept her from relaxing. Every sound brought her upright, her fingers digging into the arms of her chair, her eyes and ears fully alert. When Tremlow let the doctor in, she came to the doorway and stood as if at attention, though he hadn't even seen his patient yet. At last Dominic, worn out by *her* nerves, brought up a diversion.

"As long as we're awake, do you mind if we talk some more about Broderick's poems?" He'd reached the point where he could say her husband's name without spitting quite so obviously.

"I don't know if this is a good time . . ."

"Perhaps not. Only I had a question about something that seemed a trifle odd."

"Odd? Oh, yes, I suppose they can be rather unconventional. He wanted, you see, to invent a new kind of prosody, a new form of metrical structure."

"I wasn't referring to anything so erudite. I meant the titles."

"The titles?"

"I'll show you."

As he crossed the hall, he heard the sound of a woman's bitter sobbing from upstairs. A cold fear gripped him, exactly as though a dead hand had seized his heart. He put his hand on the newel post, preparing to leap up the stairs when a discreet cough stopped him. "I beg your pardon, Your Grace," said Tremlow.

"What's that ungodly noise?"

"Lady Danesby's maid, Your Grace, rather over-wrought."

It was against his principles to give orders to other people's servants, but this was in the nature of an emergency. "Well, silence her quickly before her ladyship hears. The last thing she needs is some banshee howling outside her door."

"Yes, Your Grace. I was about to see to the matter."

"Do so. And quietly."

When he entered the library, he gave the French doors a suspicious glance. Since the night of the burglary, he'd never felt really comfortable in this room. Not that he was windy, he hoped, but something here gave him the impression that he was being watched. He went to the doors and gave the handle a shake. It seemed that the household had begun to lock these doors and the broken pane of glass had been replaced in record time. He drew the curtains with a jerk.

Taking the box of poems from the drawer of a cabinet, Dominic returned to Sophie. "Now look at this," he said, putting the casket down in front of her and opening it quickly. "Among these stones, the sea flows, turning dull rock to jewel tones. Foam blows, taking . . ." He squinted at the page. "What's this word?"

"Wing, I think."

"First of all, if you want these to be published, someone is going to have to make a clear copy."

"Yes, I agree. Broderick's handwriting did leave something to be desired."

"That, and you never let the original copies out of your hands. It's a lesson every writer learns, usually under the worst of circumstances."

"Do you speak from experience?" she asked, able to smile with ease now that her mind was diverted.

"Bitter experience. A printer completely ruined an essay I wrote on Thomas Paine and I had given them the original and could not prove I hadn't written the thing back to front."

"Poor you. I imagine it was a good essay. He was the revolutionary agitator, wasn't he?"

"Among other things. A man who would scorn to shake the hand of a duke, but I don't think he would have minded an author. He was a fascinating man. Never had a day's luck in his life."

"You were saying something about titles. Not ducal titles, but the titles of the poems?"

Dominic brought his mind back to the problem at hand. One at least was solved: she no longer listened quite so intently for sounds from above. "Yes. Now this poem—wouldn't you think it is about the sea? Not only does it mention the sea, all the ideas are about it. Even the cadence has something oceanic about it."

"Of course it's about the sea. He wrote it in a little town on the Adriatic coast. Not Naples or Amalfi. Somewhere near there, though."

"Then why does he title it 'Where White Lilies Grow'? It doesn't make sense."

"Maybe he thought of the sea crests as white lilies. I wouldn't be surprised. His poetry is often confusing upon a first reading."

"You knew him better than I, of course. But if 'white lilies' are a metaphor for the sea crests, why doesn't he mention that image anywhere in the poem?"

"Doesn't he?" Sophie took up the piece of paper and read it, her forehead wrinkling with the effort. Dominic had to turn away to keep from smoothing it with his fingers, or his lips.

"No," she said, "you are right. That is odd. Are there any others like this? Where the title and the subject don't seem to match?"

"I haven't looked at them all, but . . ." He flipped through the sheets of paper, catching one with a juggling motion when it floated off the edge of the table. "It's this one," he said, looking at it sideways, then putting it down and reaching for another. "No, this one. 'Heart of Darkness, Heart of Stone,' whatever that may mean."

"Is it about Catherine Margrave? I'm sorry; that was uncalled for."

"On the contrary. I would say that was mild, even parliamentary, language. Most of the women I've known would have made her life a nightmare, beginning with my aunt. Even Mother might have called her 'unladylike.'"

"Is that her worst insult?"

"No, indeed. The greatest crime in her calendar is unkindness. Followed by greed."

"My mother is like that too. She used to give this little frown and shake of her head whenever Maris and I would quarrel over the last bun or some toy." She showed him.

"Charming."

"Oh, not when I was a child. I used to dread that look. Our nurse would scold or slap. All Mother had to do was to turn to either of us and *look*."

She turned her head to read the poem he'd mentioned. The subject of the poem itself seemed to describe an ideal city like Coleridge's Xanadu. Like that poem, this one was not finished or, at any rate, the poem broke off abruptly. "Is there a continuation of this one? It seems to end mid stanza."

"Is it numbered?"

She tilted the page to let the maximum amount of light fall upon it. "I think there's a number here, but it's very faint. We might be able to see it better by daylight."

A ticking noise made them look around. Tip came in, his cognac eyes seeming to ask if they had any objection to his presence. Dominic went down on one knee and Tip came up to him with a tentative wag of his plume-like tail. He seemed grateful for the attention, leaning against Dominic's leg when he stood up. "They must have overlooked him when all the excitement started upstairs."

"Poor boy, he doesn't have any idea what's happening. Do you think he'll enjoy having a baby in the house?"

"Maybe not at first," Dominic said. "But once the baby's outgrown the tail-pulling stage, they'll probably be the best of friends."

"I hope so. My father always had a dog at his heels, often more than one. I grew up feeling that a house isn't a home without a dog by the fire."

"Did you have one in Rome?"

"No. Rome is populated by stray cats. Besides, my landlord didn't allow pets in the house and Broderick . . ."

"Broderick didn't like dogs."

"Not very much."

Dominic wanted to ask if she'd known that before she'd married. Surely that dislike would have been reason enough to call off the wedding. It would have been enough for him, had he ever chosen another bride. "I am between dogs at the moment," he said, hoping this was not too obvious a comparison in his favor. "My last one— Orly—died in the spring. I'm waiting 'til his half sister has pups before choosing another."

"Do you think you could spare one for me?" Sophie

asked. "I don't think Mother would mind—that is, if I end up living at Finchley Old Place with her."

"Is there any doubt?"

"Some," she said, after a moment's hesitation. "I find that I am not as likely to slip into my old role of younger daughter and sister as I thought I would be. I think I have changed too much to go back."

"You've grown. I can understand that. When I go north to visit, both my mother and my great-aunt treat me as if I were a mere youth once more. Rather than finding it invigorating, I soon begin to chafe at it. Especially as my aunt never had a very high opinion of my good sense."

"I suppose it can't be helped," Sophie said. "We have gone into the wider world while they have stayed quietly at home, busy with their own lives. That's as it should be. But I can't go back as if nothing had ever happened. I don't want to forget either my happiness or my folly. I want to learn from them and keep on growing, not settle for a subordinate role again."

"No," Dominic said. "I can't see you as a quiet widow settled in a small English village. You should be . . ." He tried to throttle the words.

Sophie looked at him with her lovely, intelligent eyes. "Unfortunately, my choices are limited. I haven't enough funds to live as I did in Rome, nor would I if I could."

"What would you do if you could do anything?"

"Anything? Women aren't given that choice. We have only three choices—marriage, good works, or . . . well, you are a man of the world. I have been married. I cannot see myself in the third role. All that is left is good works, and I don't believe I have the temperament for it." She sighed.

"You could marry again." He saw the resigned way she

shook her head, and the sight pained him so much that he had to speak. "Yes, you could. Someone different. Someone who wouldn't want you to be smaller than you are. Someone who thinks his wife should be free to have her own thoughts, her own soul. If you wanted to look after me, if that is your idea of what a wife should be, I'd want you to. If you wanted to climb an Alp or investigate the life cycle of the common liver fluke, I'd want you to. Whatever you want, Sophie, is what I want for you."

"The common liver fluke?"

He met her eyes and they burst into laughter. He reached out and took her by the shoulders, his hands curving over her roundness. More than anything, he wanted to draw her into his arms, but he felt her stiffness and refrained. "I can offer you all the worldly things, Sophie. Great position and wealth, the admiration of fools who can only see those things. But you can give me . . ."

"What can I give you? What did you want from me before?"

"You can give me the belief that none of these things matter. If you would marry me, I could believe that you wanted only me—Dominic Swift, not the Duke of Saltaire. I need that. You've no notion how much I need it."

He saw his words sink in and felt a stir of hope. "You remembered that I said how Broderick needed me."

"I remember every word you have ever said to me."

Slowly, she stepped out of reach of his hands. "I was wrong. Broderick didn't need me, not the way I thought. If I could be so wrong about so much, how can I trust my judgment again and on the same subject?"

"You could trust mine." Even as he said it he knew that wouldn't satisfy either of them. "No," he said. "If you come to me, you must want to with your wisdom as well as your love."

"Do you think my love will be more easily won than my good sense?"

"I hope so. Napoleon taught us the futility of fighting on more than one impossible front simultaneously."

She showed him an absent smile then turned aside, her arms wrapped about her middle. "You know that I cannot say yes. I am far from ready to even contemplate such a step."

"I knew that it was too soon. But seeing you so unhappy is very difficult for me."

"Thank you. It is very comforting to know that you care. Only . . . try not to care too much."

Dominic was glad she had not looked at him. His expression would have given away even more than his words. One consolation remained. She'd turned him down twice now—if she had even the slightest interest in his title or possessions, her present condition would have tempted her to accept him. The fact that a word would alleviate all her financial difficulties and yet that word remained unspoken gave him hope that if she ever did accept him, it would be for himself alone.

He'd better change the subject.

"How much longer do you think this baby will take?" Dominic asked, knowing that with most women he would not have dared to broach such a delicate question. He felt confident that Sophie would not react missishly.

"It's hard to say. Mother told me that first children can take a very long time. But, there, I have said what prayers I can. The rest is up to God and Dr. Richards."

CHAPTER ELEVEN

Sophie saw the baby, her nephew, for the first time at eight o'clock in the morning. The late-rising winter sun had just lifted to the window, sending a beam of palest gold to touch the sleeping newborn's head. "He has hair," she marveled.

"Yes," Maris sighed, turning her head toward the basket where her baby lay. Her sweat-darkened hair clung to her forehead, and black marks nested like ravens under her eyes. But the smile upon her lips showed that whatever she had suffered, she seemed well content. "Isn't he wonderful?"

"He's so beautiful. Look at his fingers!" Sophie reached out to compare her hand with the delicate fist, wrinkled as an old man's, small as a doll's. He slept with the intense concentration that great masters give to their art.

Sophie dragged herself away from the enthralling sight of watching her nephew sleep. She came to her sister and smoothed the coverlet. "How are you feeling?"

"Tired. I don't like staying up all night, even without having a baby."

"Neither do I."

"Did you?"

"Of course. I couldn't sleep with all this going on.

But it was a productive night, though not compared with
yours. Dominic and I stayed up all night copying Broderick's poems." She didn't mention the titles they'd
changed. This was not the time to make any sort of
lengthy explanations. Besides, there were only half a
dozen or so with ill-fitting titles. Dominic had made
copies of the originals without changing anything. Surreptitiously, Sophie flexed her right hand. It still ached,
and the first knuckle of her middle finger felt raw.

Despite her exhaustion, Maris seemed on the verge of
asking some pointed questions. Sophie had no doubt
that a matchmaking plan had evolved in her sister's
brain. She cast about for something to say to distract her
but before she could think of anything, she heard a
timid rap at the door.

"See who that is, will you?" Maris asked.

Sophie opened the door and blinked in surprise.
"*Buon giorno,* Lucia. *Buon giorno,* Angelina."

Both girls nodded shyly. Between them, in their four
hands, they carried a remarkable construct. Pyramidal
in shape, it had three crosspieces loaded with fruit and
flowers, the latter twisted out of paper. Ribbons cascaded from the peak, some of which Sophie recognized
as ones she had discarded while still living in Rome.

"*Abbiano un regalo per il bambino,*" Lucia said softly
with an anxious glance into the room.

"What does she say?" Maris struggled up onto her elbows.

"They have a present for the baby."

"Ask them to come in."

"*Entrata, per favore.*" Sophie pushed the door open
wide and the girls carried in their creation, Lucia walking backward. Quickly, Sophie cleared a space on top of
a low chest. The maids laid their creation down with
great care, tweaked a ribbon, and adjusted a flower.

Then, from pockets in apron and dress, came tiny figurines of olive wood and gilt. They had the realism and perfection of Renaissance art. Sophie saw at once that these were valuable antiques. Mary, Joseph, wise men, camel, ass, sheep, and shepherds all took their places on the bottom tier. Finally, and with some crossing of themselves, the girls slipped the figure of Infant Jesus into his tiny manger.

"What is it?" Maris asked. "It's so beautiful. I've never seen anything like it."

"It's called a *creppo*. Every family makes them at Christmastime every year. Sometimes they get very elaborate. I've seen some seven feet tall."

"It's stunning. Please, how do you say 'thank you'?"

"*Grazie*."

"Then *grazie* very much."

The two girls dipped curtsies. Then Lucia asked if they could see the baby. Maris agreed, once the request was translated, and they hurried over to the bassinet to ooh and aah in a way that required no translation at all.

When Angelina looked up, her face transformed by a more brilliant smile than she usually showed, Sophie saw her red cheek, the flesh swollen and proud, a line of dried blood showing along the edge of the cheekbone. "Angelina, what happened?"

Her hand crept to cover the mark. Lucia stepped between her and the Englishwomen. "Nossing," she said. "*Cosa può farci se è stupida*."

"She says her sister can't help being . . . stupid." Bit by bit, with confirmation from Angelina, the story came out. A strange house, a dark night, a girl too lazy to light a candle, a trip in the dark, and an open door. They apologized for troubling anyone and insisted that a doctor would be unnecessary. Angelina was bathing it with arnica and vowed that the swelling was already much reduced.

After a little more baby worship, Sophie suggested that Maris needed her rest. Angelina nodded and took her sister by the hand. But Lucia had something else she wanted to say. Sophie listened and shook her head. "*È niente.*"

Maris asked what she'd said. "She is apologizing for not having fresh flowers for the *creppo*. She didn't realize that England was a land without flowers."

"Tell her that we shall have a beautiful spring and if she wishes to see flowers before then, Lord Danesby will be happy to show her the greenhouses."

Lucia beamed brightly upon hearing this from Sophie. "She says that she hasn't felt warm since she left home."

"Poor thing. I'll mention it to Kenton. He'll be thrilled to have a chance to show off his flowers to a new audience."

After the girls had gone out, Sophie came to the bedside again and took her sister's hand. "Where's that fancy nurse you hired?"

"In bed with a bruised tailbone and a bad case of irritability."

"You don't seem terribly upset about her dereliction of duty."

"Oh, I'm not. She would have taken Baby and I wouldn't see him except at her discretion. Now I can be with him all day. I'm tired, but I'm so happy."

Sophie bent down and kissed her forehead. "Congratulations. I am almost as happy as you are."

She walked down the hall, pensively. She'd never seen anything in all the world so beautiful as her nephew. Sad to think she'd never have any children of her own. Then she paused between steps, finally struck by a good reason to marry Dominic. She had no doubt that his children would be singularly good looking, with his height and undoubted attractions of person. Many women had married for less sensible reasons.

Another step on, however, Sophie had discarded the notion. He wouldn't be satisfied with such a marriage. To tell the truth, neither would she. It must be her exhaustion that led her to consider for so much as an instant such an outrageous notion.

Everyone slept half the day and wandered downstairs, unsure of whether or what they wanted to eat. Kenton wore a dazed expression, reminiscent of his wedding day, when he looked as if he'd been struck on the head by a piece of falling masonry. Now he sat at the head of the table in the morning room, smiling down at his plate as though it were a crystal ball showing him entrancing visions of his future.

Sophie sat down, meeting Dominic's eyes across the table. "Have you seen the baby?"

"Not yet. I'm not very adept with babies. They tend to cry when they look at me."

"I'm sure they don't."

"You'll see. I rather dread the christening. By the way, Kenton . . . Kenton?" He looked at his friend, who had suddenly chuckled.

He smiled at the two of them. "I've got a son," he said.

"So I hear tell," Dominic said. "What are you going to name him?"

"We could never make up our minds. William Hugh or Charles John. If it had been a girl, we were going to name her after our mothers but now . . ." Though he was obviously tired to the nth degree, he still bore a grin that seemed to have become permanent. "I'll ask Maris which one she thinks fits him, now that he's here."

He pushed back his chair to stand up but staggered as

if his legs were too weak to support him. Instantly, Dominic stood and grasped Kenton by the elbow, holding him up. "To bed with you, old man. This time, you'll sleep." Over his shoulder, he looked at Sophie. "Ask Tremlow for a glass of something. He'll sleep the better for a little sip of alcohol."

Tremlow remained his usual sagacious self, despite having had no more sleep than the rest of them. "I shall concoct my famous punch, madam. It has sent many a gentleman to sleep."

"It sounds ideal. He's so excited I doubt he can sleep otherwise. By the way, is my mother awake?"

"Yes, madam. She has only this moment gone up to visit the nursery."

Sophie didn't know whether Tremlow's face expressed some emotion, however briefly, or if she had begun to develop the knack of reading his countenance. Whichever it was, she sensed trouble.

The nursery was on the top floor in a lamp-filled room distempered a soothing blue. The fire flickered in the small fireplace, outlined in delft tiles. Heavy curtains kept the room warm. Sophie tugged at the collar of her dress.

"And I can assure you, Mrs. Lindel, that none of my other ladies had such an irregular household," Sophie heard a petulant voice say. The month-nurse lay back on a chaise, a vinaigrette in her limp hand. "These midnight disturbances, strange men rampaging through the halls, this restlessness on the part of her ladyship could have had the worst effects on the child. You have no notion how much danger that baby was in."

"I don't? On the contrary, I'm well aware of how dangerous childbirth can be. I lost a child once."

"You did?" Sophie said in amazement.

Her mother turned abruptly with a flick of skirt. "I didn't see you."

"What is this?"

"I came up to ask Simms why she isn't doing her duty."

Sophie saw the look she had described to Dominic turned, thank heavens, upon someone else. Simms melted as quickly as butter in the sun. She put her feet on the floor, feeling for her shoes, and stood up, wincing a little.

"Everything is ready for the baby, Mrs. Lindel. I'll just go down and get it."

Sophie tugged her mother's sleeve. "No," she whispered. "Maris is happier keeping the baby with her."

"She may feel that way now, but she needs her rest."

"Couldn't we help her? I'm not doing anything except eating and sleeping, and you have lots of experience with infants."

"Not for twenty years. One grows rusty. No, Simms has been hired to perform a service. She had better be about it."

When they were alone, Sophie turned to her mother. "What's this you said?"

"Oh, I'm not going to bother my children with ancient history." Seeing perhaps that Sophie wasn't about to give up, Mrs. Lindel sighed resignedly. "It was a very long time ago. Before Maris. Our first child was a boy. He lived three weeks."

"But . . . you've never said a word. You've never visited a grave . . ."

"It was a very long time ago," Mrs. Lindel said again. "We were in London at the time. He was buried in Town at St. Clement Dane. I went there the last time I visited Maris and Kenton." She smiled with understanding at her daughter. "The grave was gone. They don't keep them, you know. London cemeteries are so crowded that they move or cover over the bodies. And he was so very small."

Sophie put her arm about her mother's shoulders, more for her own comfort than because Mrs. Lindel seemed to stand in need of it. "I had no notion."

"No, there was no reason for you to know. Maris came and then you. Besides, one forgets such things. They are like a story you read once upon a time. Whether it made you laugh or cry, eventually you put it down and the details fade. You go on with your life and you say 'Well, this is what I have. I can be happy.' And you are happy."

She patted Sophie's hand, where it lay on her comfortable waist. "Oh, I forgot to tell you in all the excitement. Your gown has come. Dear Miss Bowles must have slaved like a Turk over her needle. I'd like you to try it on. You can see mine at the same time. I think it suits me. Dark blue, you know, shot with silver. I wear it with a turban."

"A turban? No, that's for dowagers. You are far too young for such things."

Mrs. Lindel's laughter did have something girlish in the tone, despite everything. "I'm so glad you came home, Sophie. Between you and your sister, you will keep me young."

"No turbans?"

"No. No turbans. Though it is very grand."

"We'll give it to Simms to reconcile her to the hardness of her lot."

The next day, the household returned to its usual schedule. Dominic and Sophie were once again in the library, copying out Broderick's poems. They had dis-

cussed the changes to the poems with the ill-fitting titles and had agreed, more or less, on what the new titles
should be. All but one.

"This passes me," Sophie said. "I can make neither
head nor tail of it. The poem is plain enough, simply
history, but why call it that?"

"The title does seem portentous," Dominic conceded.
He held the paper closer to his eyes as if that would help
bring it into focus. "I just don't know of what."

Sophie looked up at a shadow she glimpsed out of the
corner of her eye. "Kenton," she called. Her brother-
in-law straightened up, rather sheepishly, and put down
the brogues he held in his hand. His feet wore only
stockings.

"Good morning. I didn't want to disturb you."

"You were sneaking out, sir," Sophie said. Dominic
slued around in his chair to look over his shoulder with
a wide grin.

"Kenton will never make a poet."

"On the contrary," Kenton said, stung. "I wrote an ode
to my wife shortly after we were married. It even
rhymed, pretty well, though I couldn't think of anything
to rhyme with bo . . . well," he concluded with a glance
at Sophie. "Well, some of the words were difficult."

"Good," Sophie said with satisfaction. "You can come
and help us."

"Ordinarily, only too happy to help, but I must see to
my greenhouses. I haven't been down there since the
baby came, and I don't trust my gardener or, at any rate,
only as far as I can see him. He doesn't water enough."

"Just come and listen for a moment," Sophie pleaded.
"Dominic and I want your opinion on this poem."

With evident reluctance, Kenton padded over to them
in his stocking feet. He stood behind Dominic's chair,

his arms folded on the studded edge, ready for instant flight given half a chance. "Is it one of Broderick's?"

"Yes. It's called 'Walk Sunset Down' and it has us in a quandary. What do you think it means?" She cleared her throat.

> *Beatrice Cenci ate flowers*
> *to sweeten her breath,*
> *purple-lipped and deadly,*
> *a bloom withered untimely.*
> *So fair and alone in grief,*
> *waiting for time's last beat,*
> *white-handed . . .*

Kenton held up his hand. "Who's Beatrice Cenci?"

"What do you mean?" Dominic asked. "You own the play. I saw it." He unfolded his length from the chair and stepped to the shelves. "Here it is," he said, holding up a book covered in pale, limp leather. "*The Cenci,* by Percy B. Shelley. Published last year."

"Was it really?" Sophie asked. "Oh, dear. Maybe we should leave this one out then. It might suffer from comparison."

"No, don't worry about that." Dominic opened the cover, then shot Kenton a laughing glance. "Pages uncut, I see. Still ordering your books by the linear foot, old man?"

"I don't read plays; I prefer to watch them. Has it been put on?"

"I doubt it. It would be a beast to stage." He tossed the book to Kenton, who caught it handily. "Beatrice Cenci was known as the 'beautiful parricide.' With the help of a few friends and relations, she dispatched her monstrously cruel father in 1570 or thereabouts. She was executed and was lucky not to have been tortured to death. They were a fairly brutal bunch back then."

"As opposed to now?" Sophie asked. "I wonder if we will be seen as particularly brutal when people look back."

"Well, be that as it may," Kenton said. "Unless this poem mentions sunsets at some point, it seems rather odd to call it . . . what is it?"

"'Walk Sunset Down,'" Sophie said. "Maybe it is a reference to her last walk to the scaffold?"

"Why don't you just call it 'Beatrice Cenci' and not worry about it anymore?"

Dominic and Sophie looked at him in some amazement. "We didn't think of it," Dominic admitted.

Sophie held out her hand for Shelley's book. "This publisher," she said, tracing the name on the frontispiece. "O. and J. Ollier, Vere Street, Bond Street, London. Are they any good?"

"They have the reputation of being honest and no slower to pay than anyone else."

"Excellent. I shall send them the manuscript as soon as we are finished with it. After all, if they'll publish a hack like Percy Shelley, they'll surely jump at the chance to put Broderick's poems before the public."

"Before we do that," Dominic said, "I wonder if you would object to my sending a copy to an old friend of mine. He's a writer, not a poet, but a very clever and clear-minded man. Confidentially, he was a spy during the war."

"Sounds intriguing," Sophie said.

"He's married to a charming girl with two exquisite children," Dominic added quickly.

Sophie smiled without letting him see. Was he suffering from jealousy after so careless a comment?

"Philip LaCorte?" Kenton asked.

"Yes. You met him some years ago at my miserable flat in Islington. He's writing again now that he's married with a family to support. You might have read something by him," Dominic added, turning to Sophie.

"I don't recognize his name."

"He writes exotic romances. His last one was called . . ." He squinted horribly with the effort of remembering. "Oh, it was set in Sicily, which is why I thought you might have read it. *The Queen of the Volcano* or something like that."

"No, I don't think so," she said as Kenton said, "That sounds like a book for me. None of this 'beautiful parricide' stuff. No offense intended, Sophie, but it sounds more than a little morbid to me to dwell on such subjects."

"None in the world," she reassured him. "And Broderick was often morbid. As it turned out, he was quite right. He did not live to be old." She looked at their faces and wanted to tell them, especially Kenton, not to hang his head abashed. But, what with his son being born, she felt it was not time to add to his shocks. "Why do you want to send a copy of the manuscript to this Mr. LaCorte?"

"Mostly to garner another opinion as to the merits of the poetry. You are prejudiced because you believe Broderick Banner was a great poet. I'm prejudiced because I . . ." He paused, glancing sideways at Kenton, who listened with great attention. "Don't you have flowers to water?"

"And Maris says I don't understand hints," Kenton said. "Very well. Keep your secrets. I may say I don't envy either of you, copying out such stuff as that, like so many medieval monks copying the Bible."

Sophie saw Dominic surreptitiously flex his right hand. She smiled up at him, wishing she could find words to tell him of her gratitude. The situation between them could have been so very awkward if it weren't for the grace and sympathy he'd shown. She fought with her own sense of embarrassment in his presence, forcing herself to remain casual and friendly when she would have liked to blush and hide her face.

"Actually, Kenton, I'm glad I caught you," Dominic said. "I don't wish to treat your house like a hotel, but I want to deliver these poems to Philip as quickly as I can and not wait for the post."

"Come and go as you like, you know that," Kenton said. "Maris says she likes it when you are here. Keeps me from hanging on her neck." He saluted Dominic lazily with two fingers and went off, whistling.

"Do you think your friend will like these poems?" Sophie asked, idly stirring the ink with the point of her pen.

"I think he will find them most interesting. I'm taking the ones with the original titles, if that's acceptable."

"Of course. As you know, I have some doubts about changing the titles. Broderick didn't care whether the masses understood his work or not. He said if he couldn't make people feel, he'd settle for making them think."

"You admired him very much," Dominic said. He had a way of standing that made him appear very relaxed, as if he had a wall to prop him up even when he stood alone in the center of the floor.

"Of course." She laid down her pen. "I wish you would tell me . . ."

"What?"

"It's ridiculous. You know my entire emotional history. I was young and foolish and fell in love with a stranger whom I invested with every virtue and quality." Her tone poured scorn upon the commonplace phrase.

"You even claim to wish to marry me. Yet I know nothing whatever about you beyond the barest facts. You love your mother and cordially dislike your great-aunt. You have a genie of the ring masquerading as your servant and a good man for a friend. Yet what about *your* past loves? I hope they are as innumerable as grains of sand on a beach and as widely scattered."

"Do you truly wish to know?" Dominic abandoned his relaxed pose and came to lean forward over the writing desk they'd been sharing. His eyes seemed larger and brighter than she'd ever seen them.

Sophie nodded. "Yes. I do."

"Well, then . . ." He opened his mouth as if to launch into a catalog but stopped and straightened. "No, I don't think I will. If you really want to know everything, marry me and I'll take you to see Great-Aunt Clementina. She'll fill your ears with all the gossip."

"Then there is gossip?" Sophie nodded wisely. "I thought there must be."

"There's always gossip. It is as constant as wind and blows just as much dust in your eyes. But no one can deny that it is most interesting at times."

"That's two good reasons for marrying you. If I come up with a third, I just might consent." Sophie spoke lightly but couldn't resist glancing at him to see his expression. She half suspected she'd see appalled horror in his eyes, but instead she surprised an expression that she recognized. Desire, bright as a flame, danced in his blue eyes. To her astonishment and with no particular sense of welcome, she recognized the same feeling in herself. She dragged her gaze away from his mouth the instant she realized she was staring at it.

"What was your first reason?" he asked, his voice soft and husky.

"I . . ."

"You said you had two good reasons for marrying me."

"I misspoke."

"I see." A little blindly, he turned again toward the books, running his fingertips over the spines, but not as if he saw the titles.

"Will you be gone for very long?"

"I doubt it. He lives about forty miles from here. I'll break my journey at a little inn I know. The whole visit shouldn't take more than four or five days, depending on the weather."

"You'll drive, of course."

"No," he said, walking to the window. He looked out. "The weather is clearing. I'll ride. The horse needs the exercise and, frankly, so do I. Mrs. Lemon might be squeamish, but she's a marvelous cook."

"My mother says there is to be a party at the home of Mr. Lively. It is quite the event of the Christmas season, if you'd care to return for it."

"Oh, is he giving it again? I went one year with Kenton before he was married. Yes, I shall certainly return in time for that. Will you save me a dance or two?"

"I will. I'll be happy to."

CHAPTER TWELVE

After Dominic left, Sophie kept as busy as possible. She spent time leaning over the cradle, gazing at her nephew. Simms tried several times to assert her absolute authority, but the irregularity of the household was too much for her. Sophie encouraged her brother-in-law to pick up his own son, despite Simms's objections. Maris, under orders to stay in bed for ten days, arose on the third day after her child's birth, though Kenton insisted on carrying her up and down the stairs.

She would sit in the library, close to the fire, sewing lace caps for the baby while Sophie copied out the poems. There were forty-seven in all. Fifteen or so would probably be cut before publication. Though they had some good images or phrases, the overall quality was not Broderick's best. The seven poems with strange titles were an interesting mix. Three were splendid. The other four, including "Walk Sunset Down," seemed a trifle trite, as if they were imitations of another's work rather than the pure product of Broderick's mind.

She came across the one that was about her and her wedding day. Dominic had argued for its inclusion, but Sophie still hesitated over sharing that poem with the world. It brought everything back so clearly. The perfume of an evening in an English spring had filled the air, the moonlight and the trees seeming to whisper sweet conspiracies to one another. Dominic—that is—*Broderick* had kissed her with such tender emotion, such breathless yearning . . .

"Sophie?" Maris said, breaking in upon her thoughts. "Sophie? You've been sitting there for five minutes with your pen in the air. The ink must have dried hard by now."

"I'm sorry. My thoughts were a million miles away. Did you say something?"

"No. I was only afraid you'd gone off in an apoplexy with me sitting right here. What were you thinking of? Broderick?"

"Yes. Broderick."

Maris finished basting the ribbon around the edge of the cape and began feather-boning it. "I did like him, you know. I could see why a well-read young lady would fall in love with him. He did have a way with him. The way he'd look at you during a dinner party as if you were the most intelligent and beautiful woman he'd ever met. Of course, he'd look the same way at the woman sitting on his other side, but there's no doubt it was flattering while it lasted."

"Did he do that? I hadn't noticed." Surely, she must have noticed at some point that Broderick had, like Henry V, "largesse universal, like the sun, his liberal eye doth give to every one." There had been those girls, when she'd first met him in Yorkshire, who had hung upon his every word, even as she herself was guilty. He had declared them children and swore he gave no thought to them. If she had doubted him, his attitude was so noble in forgiving her that her jealousies had been quieted by shame.

"He did choose me in the end," Sophie said.

"Yes, he did," Maris agreed with a soft smile. "Mother and I wondered why."

"Thank you very much, indeed." She feigned indignation.

"Now, you know I didn't mean it that way. You were very lovely."

"A pity I've gone down so quickly. A mere three years and I'm an antidote." But she quite failed to keep the laughter out of her voice.

"There, I knew you weren't angry," Maris said with a pleased sigh. "It's only that we wondered whether Broderick had designs on your fortune."

"Fortune? Of course not. I have none to be coveted. Are you feeling quite yourself, Maris?"

"Didn't he meet you while you were visiting Uncle Shirley? A very wealthy man with no heirs. What could be more logical than that he should leave his fortune to us? And there is Kenton. You know what sort of a man he is—generous, thoughtful, caring. Would he let his wife's sister's family go into debtor's prison?"

"I see." Sophie reflected for a moment. "No, you misjudge Broderick. Money meant nothing to him. As long as he had enough to buy a coffee at the Caffè Greco when it suited him and a few pence for a new goose quill, he was a happy man. He married me because he loved me; when he loved me no longer, he left me. That's the way he was. If I went on loving him a little longer than was sensible, that was too bad. He felt sorry for me, but one does not return to a wife out of pity."

"Then he was immoral, and I thought him only grasping."

"He was a poet," Sophie said and returned to her work.

An hour later, after Maris had retired for her afternoon nap, Sophie finished the last line of a poem and paused to read it over. Every word must be exactly as Broderick wrote it. She'd heard too many poets complain that their copyists had been careless, turning rooks into books and haste to waste.

Her mother came in, somewhat flustered. "Here's a fine thing. Tremlow's just informed me that someone has stolen half a ham out of the kitchen. Half a ham!"

"How did they manage that?"

"The kitchen was left empty for a few minutes when Mrs. Lemon went down to the cellar. She'd brought up the ham for tonight's dinner but had forgotten that she needed a new jar of that fancy French mustard Kenton is so partial to. When she came back, the ham was gone."

"Could Tip have taken it? He's a good dog, but the best of us can be tempted."

"I beg your pardon, madam," Tremlow said, entering with tread so stately one instinctively glanced behind him for the sweep of an ermine robe. "I have ascertained that Tip is asleep on the master's dressing gown in his room. There is no trace of ham bone, either visually or olfactorily. I believe this to be the work of a human agency."

"Have any of the stable lads been especially hungry lately, Tremlow?"

"Not to my knowledge, madam. I shall, of course, investigate. I wonder, however, if you would condescend to ask the young Italian girls if they have seen it."

"Oh, I'm sure they wouldn't steal a ham, but I shall ask them if they saw anything suspicious in the kitchen."

Mrs. Lindel asked a question. "Were there any footprints in the snow?"

"The walkway was swept with unusual care this morning by young Elden. Naturally, I do not wish to reprimand the boy for his zeal, though I could have wished this morning saw him sweeping in his more indolent fashion."

Sophie felt a certain reluctance to ask the Ferrara girls about the ham. She had never heard a word against either of them and, in their small Roman neighborhood, she would. Whatever gossip Dominic promised was as nothing compared with the epic quality of the gossiping women in her former neighborhood.

She knocked on their door, determined to exercise the utmost in tact. However, her resolution proved useless. No one answered her rapping.

Sophie tried the handle. The door opened. Peering into the room, she saw that it was indeed empty of people. Two beds, one rather larger than the other, stood against the far wall, matching crucifixes hanging over the iron-frame heads. A white china ewer and basin stood on a dark oaken stand with a small tilting mirror on top. A small fireplace showed banked coals. The curtains were open over the little windows, showing the tops of the trees at the edge of the garden. The wind was blowing, sending a fine silt of blown snow flying like magic sparkles through the air.

The room was no different than a thousand other servants' quarters, only as comfortable as necessary. Perhaps Finchley could be considered as dull compared to Rome, where the very walls breathed long history and every step outside could lead to adventure.

Sophie felt a stab of guilt that she had not taken more care of the girls since returning home, so caught up in her own questions about her future. It wasn't right. Though their parents had insisted their daughters accompany her, she had accepted the responsibility. Though her mother and the upper servants had taken on the role of teaching them how to go on in England, ultimately their adjustment was her duty.

She went down to the lower level of the house. "I beg your pardon, Mrs. Lemon . . ."

"Mrs. Banner? What may I do for you?"

"Have you seen the Ferrara girls? Mr. Tremlow thought they were in their room, but they're not."

"Aren't they, indeed? I confess I find it difficult to make out what they're saying, but I thought that's where they were going."

Sophie pressed her hands together, palm to palm. "About this missing ham, Mrs. Lemon . . ."

"A fine ham, well-smoked, from Gilling's farm, not half cut. I could have done wonderful things with that ham." She seemed to mourn culinary wonders that would now never be conjured from her kitchen.

"What do you think happened to it?"

"I think the same ruffian who broke into the library came in here. Some nasty tramp looking for whatever he could steal. A objet de art, one of them silver statues, a ham, it's all the same. Lucky we weren't all murdered in our beds."

"I suppose that's true."

"I'm sleeping with the big cleaver under my pillow," Mrs. Lemon said with ferocious pride.

Considering how Mrs. Lemon fainted at the very sound of the word "blood," Sophie doubted if she could actually use a cleaver on an intruder, even if she did use one on dinner.

"I'm sure that's a good idea," Sophie said reassuringly. "But I'll have a word with Lord Danesby. Maybe he can have the stable lads guard the house."

"It'll be a bitter cold night, ma'am. I'd better start tea and hot soup. Split pea 'n' . . . no, that won't do. Maybe a nice chicken stew." She began ticking off ingredients on her fingers.

Sophie, beginning to grow concerned, went looking

for Tremlow. "I can't find the Ferrara girls. Do you know where they've gone to?"

This time, she had no difficulty reading his feelings. She could tell he didn't know as soon as she asked. The knowledge that he did not know something about his own household rocked him. "I will find out, madam."

Kenton agreed that measures should be taken to secure the house, though he obviously didn't believe a stolen ham merited so much security. He felt so even less when Mrs. Lindel professed that she'd forgotten that the Ferrara girls had asked permission to go for a walk into the village. "They said they wanted something, but Lucia didn't seem to know the word for it."

Sophie didn't like to criticize her mother, but no one else spoke. "You let them go alone?"

"They are not alone. They have each other and Finchley is hardly a sink of iniquity."

Sophie admitted the justice of this. "I don't know why I'm so nervous. So much has happened so quickly, I can't keep pace with events."

"Perhaps you are still accustoming yourself to being at home. Also, you have worked so hard on these poems. Why don't you lie down for a little? I will bring you a cup of my special herb tea."

Not even three years had dimmed her memories of her mother's "special tea." She could tell from Kenton's expression that he had had a dose of it at least once.

"Actually," she said hastily, "I think I will finish what I have to do. I'd like this to go to the post tomorrow and I still have the letter to the publishers I must write."

But when she was alone, she didn't immediately take up her pen. She felt restless and out of sorts and had not Maris's good excuse for these feelings. Focusing on writing praise of her late husband's work was an activity which engendered no enthusiasm. It required a close and focused examination of her true feelings. If Dominic had been there, she could have used him for a sounding board, however unfair such a role might be for a man who confessed to want her for his wife.

Sophie tossed down her pen and resolved to go for a walk herself. She could always claim that she went to smooth the Ferrara sisters' path in Finchley.

The weather had warmed, despite the breeze that flapped at the skirt of her heaviest dress and Maris's fur-lined pelisse. Yet the bracingly cold wind seemed to sweep the cobwebs from her brain. She began to walk more quickly, her arms swinging freely. Her mother was wrong. She didn't need more rest, she needed more exercise, more freedom. And yet, even as she exerted herself, she felt as though someone walked beside her. Not the ghost of her husband, crying at her shoulder, bidding her to remember or to forgive. This shade was taller, kinder, and more joyful. But Sophie refused to look for this phantom. She wanted to walk her own way, not chained anymore to her own betraying wishes.

Sophie stopped into Mr. Harley's shop, the only source in Finchley for those thousands of necessities of great use but not valuable enough to be specially ordered from the metropolis. Since Kenton's marriage, he'd begun to carry a "choicer" line of goods and to wear a cherry-red damask waistcoat, a gold chain stretched across an increasing waistline. The mingled fragrances of spice, toilet water, and apples swept Sophie back to her childhood, when the rare penny would be spent on boiled sweets.

Mr. Harley came trotting around his counter as Sophie entered. "Miss Sophie! Miss Sophie! Mother," he called, looking over his shoulder into the back of the shop. "Mother, it's Miss Sophie!"

She hadn't expected such a daughter's welcome. True,

Mr. Harley had traded with her family for years and Mrs. Harley had taught her to knit when no one else had been able to drill the rudiments into her head.

Mr. Harley seized her gloved hands. "How do you do?"

"Very well, thank you. I'm very glad to be home. I have missed Finchley very much."

"Certainly Finchley has missed you," he said, beaming like a stout lighthouse.

Mrs. Harley came out from the rear of the shop, flicking aside the curtain that separated the public and private venues. "There you are. Father and I were just wondering when we'd see you. You weren't in church."

"No, I'm afraid I overslept."

"There now, isn't that just what we said, Father? Young people need their rest. Would you like a cup of tea? I baked yesterday," she said in the tone of the serpent in the Garden.

"Thank you, but no. I only came in to ask if you had . . ."

"Hungary Water?" Mr. Harley said eagerly. "Florida Water? Essence of Persia?"

"Nothing, thank you. I came to ask if you had seen two young girls, blond, pretty . . . they speak very little English."

The Harleys exchanged a glance. "No, not today," he said. "They came in two days ago to buy some basilicum powder and an ounce of pipe tobacco . . . Mr. Tremlow's kind."

"Two days ago?"

"Didn't they have permission?" Mrs. Harley said, clicking her tongue chidingly. "They seemed like such nice girls, even though I couldn't understand hardly a word. They took tea."

"No, they didn't have permission to come to the village. I'm sure no harm was done. They aren't used to the restrictions of good service." She paused a moment. "They didn't come in again today?"

"No, Miss Sophie. That was the only time I've seen them," Mr. Harley said.

Mrs. Harley echoed him. Then, as if this were what she'd wanted to say all along, said, "I hope all is well with her la'ship and the dear little one?"

"Yes, indeed. Maris is recovering nicely and the baby is as sweet as can be."

She smiled like the grandmother she was. "The dear little thing. And a boy. This is the best news we could have had. There's been a Danesby in Finchley since I don't know when. So lovely to know the line will continue."

"Yes, indeed," Mr. Harley said, nodding like a mandarin. "Excellent for Finchley to know there will always be a Danesby here."

They seemed to be taking rather a lot for granted. She could think of a hundred ways in which Danesbys would be gone from Finchley in a month, let alone a hundred years. But if thinking otherwise made them happy, she would not damage their confidence.

"We are delighted that he is so healthy and strong. His cries could wake the dead."

The draper and grocer chuckled. "Now then, that's what we like to hear," he said.

"Bless me, I all but forgot!" Holding her apron in two hands, Mrs. Harley hurried away out of sight behind the curtain. She came back in an instant, a soft package in her hand, white cloth wrapped up with a pale pink ribbon. "This is for the little love with all our remembrances," she said, pressing it into Sophie's hand. "Just a little knitted jacket to keep off the cold."

"Thank you, Mrs. Harley. I know Maris will love it. I must be off."

They came to the door to wave good-bye. Sophie didn't dare show hesitation in choosing a direction. She set off up the street. Glancing behind her, she saw that the Harleys had gone in, though it didn't mean they weren't watching her from behind the narrow shop windows. She stepped into the apothecary's.

Strangely, no one else in Finchley had ever noticed the two girls. Sophie began to have the feeling that the two Italian maids were a shared hallucination, with herself as the center. Maybe she hadn't brought them back with her. Horrors, perhaps her family and the Harleys were only humoring her, as one did with people who had strayed from the path of reality. Even she recognized that she'd been behaving rather oddly. Any sane woman would have leaped at the chance to be Duchess of Saltaire.

Therefore, when she glimpsed another face she knew, she nearly dismissed it as a figment of a disordered mind. What could Clarence Knox want in Finchley? She turned to watch the man enter the Royal Oak and started to cross the street, but two horsemen passed in front of her and she lost sight of the man for a moment. When she reached the inn, she saw the courtyard was empty except for a boy sweeping the yard. "Did a stranger come through the gate just now?"

"No, ma'am. I haven't seen a soul 'cept for you and Mr. Pye, a gentleman come to wet his whistle."

"How long ago did he come in?"

The boy squinted up at the clock above the stableyard. Why, Sophie did not know, as it stopped working twenty years ago. "Must be an hour or so now, ma'am."

"Thank you," she said, fishing a penny from her pocket. "Maybe I am going mad," she murmured.

"Ma'am?"

"Never mind. Thank you."

Sophie did not care for mysteries. The world seemed complex enough without people making difficulties. As soon as she returned home, she would ask the Ferrara girls not to go to Finchley without asking. It simply wasn't wise to disappear like this, especially as they did not know their way very well. If they became lost, they could easily flounder in a snowdrift or be lost in the woods.

Her first action, however, was to give Maris Mrs. Harley's gift. Maris sat up on the edge of her bed and unwrapped it and smiled down on the tiny white garment. Lifting it to her cheek, she rubbed it there, enjoying the softness of the wool. "Look at this pattern. It's so pretty."

"You're lucky. She doesn't give much of her work away."

"Yes, I bought several things at the last church sale. I snatched this pair of pillowcases right from under Mrs. Pike's hand. She resumed speaking to me, eventually." Maris ran a finger along the hand-crocheted edge of the pillowcase.

Sophie smiled. "Tell me, Maris. How did you adjust to this house and this position you hold? You weren't born to be the mistress of a manor."

"Oh, I don't know . . ." Maris put her chin up and looked down her nose. "Give me a lorgnette and a pigeon chest and I will look like every dowager duchess I know."

"What about the Dowager Duchess of Saltaire?"

"I haven't met her. Dominic says she doesn't wish to interfere with his pleasures."

"What pleasures? He doesn't seem to enjoy being a duke."

"I can understand that. I don't enjoy being Lady Danesby. What I enjoy is being married to Kenton. The rest—the house, the people who curtsy, the money— that's enjoyable for a while. Very enjoyable," she added, with a reminiscent smile. "But none of it would be worth anything if I were married to anyone else."

"Still, how did you learn to . . ."

"Order people around?"

"Yes, I suppose that's what I mean."

"Kenton told me that if I meant what I said every time I spoke to a servant, then I would never have any trouble. I've found that to be good advice."

"Is it that simple?"

Maris nodded happily. "I make mistakes, often. Fortunately, the staff here is very understanding. Tremlow, of course, is a treasure."

"Would it be wrong to marry a man because he keeps a good valet?" Sophie said, half to her herself.

If Maris's eyebrows rose any farther, they would have disappeared in her hair. She opened and closed her mouth two or three times.

Sophie smiled at her. "Have you received many baby gifts?"

She asked Tremlow to tell her as soon as the Ferrara girls returned. He promised he would with an air of determination.

She sat down in the library, pulling a piece of paper toward her. She had every intention of writing a smooth, intelligent, and powerful piece of pleading. It must be a letter that would demand attention. She only wished Dominic were there to write it. Signing something "Duke of Saltaire" commanded both attention and respect.

The ink in her standish had sunk by half and she'd achieved little but a page that looked more like a sheet of music than a letter. Every paragraph had strong horizontal slashes running through the lines.

Irritated with herself, she lay down her pen and took up the poetry. Maybe she could find inspiration in Broderick's work. She'd hardly begun on the first one when a soft, butlerine cough interrupted her.

"I have them, madam."

The two girls still wore their outdoor clothing, close-fitting hats and black capes edged with broad scarlet ribbons. Except for the mark on Angelina's face, they looked just as they always did, open-eyed and innocent.

Sophie waved to them, motioning them to come closer. "Thank you, Tremlow."

He bowed. "Shall I wait?"

"There's no need. I shall explain to them that it isn't safe for them to wander off like this. They're good, sensible girls. They will understand."

"Very good, madam. I may as well say that their behavior has given rise to a certain sense of resentment among the other female staff."

"Yes. I see. Thank you, Tremlow."

Angelina had moved over to the writing desk and had begun straightening the desktop, shuffling the papers together, wiping the pen, and brushing a little spilled sand into her hand. The smile on her lips lent her a certain beauty. She seemed utterly contented to be doing this work. When Sophie spoke to her, she grew solemn, glancing often at her sister.

Looking at them, seeing them so honest, Sophie felt a great reluctance to question them about the missing ham. Though she strove for tact, for a moment she wasn't sure if Angelina would explode in anger. Lucia took her sister's hand, calming her. She said that they were both ignorant as to the ham's fate.

Sophie passed quickly on to her other subject. They both seemed to understand Sophie's difficulty when she explained it. They promised faithfully not to stray from the grounds without asking leave. She reminded them that she had only the status of guest in her sister's house. The first duty of a guest was not to alarm her hosts with avoidable difficulties. Soon, they would retire to her mother's house and new arrangements might be made, such as an extra afternoon off per week.

Lucia denied that they required so much liberty. There simply wasn't enough work here to keep them occupied as fully as they would like. The staff was "*molto rapido*"—so quick, in fact, that no sooner did something need to be done than it was done. They did enjoy working on the Christmas decorations, but so many hands made very light work.

Sophie assured them that there would soon be plenty to do. In the meantime, she promised to ask if there were any special tasks that needed doing—a pre-spring cleaning, as it were. She couldn't blame the girls for seeking more occupation. As it was, she longed for some small but satisfying work, some task that could be completed in an afternoon. She wanted to step back from a freshly painted wall or a well-sewn seam and announce that she had accomplished this.

In the meantime, however, she had a letter to write . . . again.

CHAPTER THIRTEEN

"We shouldn't put off visiting our friends any longer," Mrs. Lindel said early on Thursday morning. "I'm sure they must be wondering what we are hiding."

"Hiding?" Sophie looked up from her breakfast. "What could we be hiding?"

"Knowing our friends, anything from disfiguration to murder. I only hope Miss Bowles has been able to finish one of your day dresses, though I suppose your gown for tomorrow evening was more important. We shall stop by to check on her progress."

"Thank heaven for the custom of not allowing a new mother out in public until she has been churched," Maris said, with a laughing glance at her husband. "They are welcome to gossip about me as much as they choose."

"As if they could," Kenton replied gallantly.

"Believe me, they can. But listen, I haven't been entirely idle while lying in bed. I have a surprise for you, Sophie." With something of her old lightness and quickness of movement, Maris left the table, leading her sister out by the hand.

When Sophie came down again, she wore a modish carriage dress of rich blue poplin, a deep flounce of blond lace drawing attention to her feet, matched by the collar of lace at her throat. It fit her to perfection, as did the deeper blue Levantine pelisse that she wore thrown open.

If the fit were not exact, with a pelisse it did not matter so much. Sophie paused on the bottom step, posed as if for her portrait, the large muff she'd borrowed before hanging from her hand.

Maris, watching from above, clapped her hands at the expressions on her mother's and husband's faces. "Isn't that your very best bonnet?" Kenton asked.

"Yes, darling. You bought it for me."

The deep brim of the dark blue hat was lined in cream satin and came forward like blinkers over Sophie's cheeks. Three curling plumes in three shades of blue, the lightest one larger than the other two, gave her the appearance of impressive height.

"I like it on her, very much," he said consideringly. From up above, a slipper struck his shoulder, followed by a giggle. With a grin, he stooped and picked up the small black shoe. "Pardon me, ladies. Enjoy your drive."

Two at a time, he raced up the stairs, laughing. A small shriek was followed by the sound of kisses.

Sophie and Mrs. Lindel sighed indulgently. "You do look magnificent," her mother said.

"I feel magnificent, but am afraid I look as though I am playing dress-up in my big sister's clothes. It's true enough."

"On the contrary, you look as though you've always worn such things."

"I suppose, muff and all, I must be wearing thirty guineas on my back."

"Nearer seventy, my love. Kenton will have everything of the best."

"Seventy?" Sophie paused, glancing up as she debated changing into her own clothes. "I trust I won't spill anything."

Mrs. Lindel, having lived in the neighborhood for most of her adult life, had many friends. Almost nowhere could they escape with only a card left with the butler, if there was one. At every stop, they were welcomed into the house and refreshment was pressed upon them. After being plied with tea or cordial, they were then subject to questioning, all perfectly polite and thus impossible to escape. Sophie concealed the unhappiness of her marriage, not wishing to give rise to more gossip, and, at a hint from her mother, remained vague upon the exact date of Broderick's passing. When they parted at most houses, it was with the wish that they would meet again at Mr. Lively's party upon the morrow.

Only at Miss Menthrip's house did evasive tactics not avail her. "So," she said, "you've come home again and without that wastrel husband of yours. So much the better."

Miss Menthrip had changed but little. A little older, a little grayer, she leaned a trifle more heavily on a twisted stick of black ash in her low-ceilinged home. Her tongue had lost none of its sting. But Maris and Sophie had always known that a heart of butter beat under the stiff black silk. She couldn't abide cringers or mealymouthed persons. Give her as good as she gave and she would always stand friends.

"I'm not going to argue with you, Miss Menthrip," Sophie said. "My mother has taught me to respect my elders."

"Hah, think I'm too old to stick to my guns, eh? Or can't take defiance? He was a wastrel, a ne'er-do-well, a flibbertigibbet. Poet? I could write better myself."

"I will agree that he was not a good provider, as the farmers say, and perhaps we were not as happy as we could have been, for which I am in part responsible. But he was a great poet, Miss Menthrip. One day, all the world will know it."

"How?"

"I have sent his poems off to a publisher. If they do not accept them, I will try another and another until his genius is acknowledged."

"Hmmph! Fine words butter no parsnips, my lass. When do you intend to do this wonderful thing, eh?"

"I've done it already. The parcel with a copy of his poems went off this morning."

"Did it? Did it, indeed? You let no grass grow under your feet, miss, I'll say that for you," she said with the air of one snatching a single brand from the burning. "What will your new husband make of your spending so much time on the scribblings of your old one, eh?"

"New husband?" Sophie said, faltering for the first time. "What new husband?"

"How should I know? Fine as five pence you are, and if some young rascal isn't already in love with you, it must be your fault indeed."

Mrs. Lindel intervened. "She's not even out of mourning yet."

"Fine feathers," Miss Menthrip said, pointing her stick at Sophie.

"Borrowed plumage," she shot back, recovering her pluck.

"I know it, I know it," Miss Menthrip said, cackling like a parrot. "That confoundedly silly niece of mine is making your other clothes up. Pretty things too, though I don't like that very pale purple on blondes. Washes 'em out. I told her to make it out of that figured silk."

"What figured silk?" Mrs. Lindel demanded. "We saw none such."

"No, I know you didn't. That ninny forgot she had it on order. It came a day later and she didn't want to trouble you to come all the way out again. I told her, 'I've never known one of those Lindels to stay at home if they could go out,' but there, she's a fool now and time shan't mend her."

"I'll go at once. You stay, Sophie. Keep Miss Menthrip company." Mrs. Lindel hurried from the house.

"Do you care for tea?" Miss Menthrip croaked. "Put the kettle on, child."

"Truthfully, Miss Menthrip . . ."

"Truthfully, I'm the last in a long line of calls and you feel so full up of tea that you could drown. Aye, I remember. Go out and look at my garden; you'll feel the better for it."

When she came back into the house, cold but relieved, she could indeed face a cup of tea. A few meager biscuits set out on a plate she ignored. Miss Menthrip, though more secure than she'd been once upon a time, still had to count her pence or have no pounds at all. Her plates and cups might be Derby but her poverty was well known.

Tea was a comfort to poor and rich alike. They sipped in silence for a moment. "Are you very badly off?" Miss Menthrip asked in a less challenging way.

"I'm afraid so. My mother, my sister, and her husband are very kind, but I cannot live on their charity."

"Why not? I do."

Sophie, afraid she'd hurt the older woman, hastened to make her meaning clear, but Miss Menthrip held up her hand.

"Never mind, never mind. I know what you would say. Our cases are not alike. You are young and strong, well able to face the cold winds of this world. So was I, once. But one grows tired of the battle. One is glad, in the end, for kindness, even if it be charity."

"I am not come to that."

"Still, bear it in mind. Now, you say that you have sent a parcel to these publishing johnnies. Where are they?"

"London."

"London, eh? Would it surprise you very much to learn that no parcel of any description left Finchley for London today?"

Fortunately, Sophie had put down her teacup or Maris's dress would surely have been imperiled. "How do you know that?"

"Have you been gone so long you've forgotten the great interest we all take in one another?" Miss Menthrip's still-black eyebrows lifted. "I can tell you that Mrs. Alberts received her new feathers, Mr. Lanscombe his chemicals, and that both Danesby and Dr. Richards have written to London to record the birth of the heir. Miss Bowles has written her weekly letter to her sister and Susan Archer has written for new music, for which we all give thanks since we've heard 'Maiden's Lament' and 'A Scot's Farewell to Bannockburn' until we're fair sick."

"But no parcel to Messrs. Ollier in Vere Street?" Sophie knew what Miss Menthrip said was true even before she offered her proofs. Finchley as a whole did keep a close eye on what passed through Mr. Harley's hands. He had acted as postmaster here for several years. Despite his propensity for gossip, he remained the best man for the position.

"Who did you give it to? Or did you leave it on the table in the hall, as is the custom?"

Sophie wasn't surprised that Miss Menthrip knew where the mail collected at Finchley Place. She probably knew everything from how often they changed the linen to the length of Mrs. Lemon's apron strings. "I left it on the table per Mr. Tremlow's instructions."

"Then you must discover who took it from there, for I assure you it never came to town. Ask Mr. Harley, if you don't wish to take my word for it."

"You know I cannot ask him. It will be all over town in a moment. Will you promise not to tell anyone?"

"I do not pass on what I hear. I am the end of this gossip river, not its source. But you will let me know what passes?" Her eyes glittered like a habitual drunkard scenting whiskey on the air.

"As soon as I know myself," Sophie promised.

"Excellent. Also, by the way, there was a letter for you, unfranked. It should be waiting for you when you arrive at Finchley Place. Oh, look. Here comes your mother."

Sophie rode home in a brown study, answering her mother absently, infrequently, and often with ludicrous results. "Sophie, you're not listening," Mrs. Lindel said. "What has you so preoccupied?"

"I'm tired, Mother. That's all. It is exhausting visiting all these people, and my garters are digging into my legs."

"Sophie!"

"It's true."

"Then adjust them, but discreetly. I'm glad this is a closed carriage."

"Considering the weather, so am I." She made no movement toward loosening the tight garters. "What are you giving Maris for Christmas, Mother?"

"I've embroidered half a dozen handkerchiefs with her cipher upon them in blue, encircled with rose buds."

"And for Kenton?"

"Oh, Kenton is a difficult person to give anything to. He has so much and what he wants, he buys. However, Dominic suggested I purchase a new purse for him. I found one in London in Moroccan leather with a ring around the mouth. He's always dropping coins, have you noticed?"

"No, I can't say that I have. And for me?"

"For you, I have a . . . secret." Mrs. Lindel smiled at her daughter's transparent attempt to prise information from her. "You're still such a child, Sophie."

"In some things. I hope I will always try to winkle out the secret of my Christmas presents before I receive them. Can't you offer me so much as a hint?"

"Not so much as a word," Mrs. Lindel said. "I am mute."

When Sophie entered the house, she asked Tremlow where her brother-in-law might be. "He has ridden out upon business, madam. I have instructions not to wait dinner for him."

"I see." She debated a moment over asking Tremlow about the missing parcel but, fearing this might be construed as a criticism of some arrangement of the household, she held off. Maris was not available as she was sound asleep.

As Miss Menthrip had prophesied, a letter did await Sophie. As she opened it and read it, Mrs. Lindel waited. The instant Sophie had finished it, she asked, "Is it from Dominic?"

"No. Dominic has no cause to write to me. Besides, he should return today or tomorrow. No, this letter is from that Mr. Knox that I knew in Rome."

"Is that the man who went with Broderick to that island? Which one was it?"

"Sicily. Yes, he was Broderick's dearest friend and was there when he died."

"I'm glad he wasn't alone. What does Mr. Knox write?"

"He has found work as a tutor to several young men making their try for University."

"That doesn't sound very steady."

"He was recommended to the position by a cousin who promises him a position in his bank come the spring. Mr. Knox is uncertain whether it will suit him. He has a poetic soul and such men do not worship easily in the temples of Mammon."

"Does he write that?" her mother asked incredulously.

"No," Sophie said and added, with a wicked smile, "Mr. Knox did me the honor of confiding in me during our homeward journey."

"If he's wise, he'll take what he can and trouble less about his soul. These are not times for men without situation."

"Are there ever such times?" She put down the letter. "It is wrong, however, for him to leave Kenton to pay for his letter. I suppose I'd better answer, though that isn't fair to Kenton, either."

"Dear Kenton isn't the sort to count such matters. Nevertheless, I can't say I think Mr. Knox an acquaintance worth pursuing."

"I've no intention of pursuing him, Mother," Sophie said seriously. "He's Broderick's friend. When he told me about his death, I'd never seen anyone so devastated by grief."

"But you said he first visited Broderick's . . ." she almost couldn't form the word.

"Yes, he did. But he was shaking and crying when he told me. I can't simply cut the connection as if he were perfectly unknown to me."

"No, that wouldn't be right. However, there's no need to reply at once. Wait a week or so."

"Yes, I suppose that would be best. You know, I honestly thought I saw . . ."

"Listen, is that the gong?"

Tremlow had ceased striking the dinner gong with all his strength, as it invariably woke the baby even though the nursery was at the rear of the house. With his usual dedication, he achieved a pianissimo trembling of the gong that resembled the fluttering heartbeat of a dove rather than the Jovian thunder of old. Though the baby slept undisturbed, the adults found it difficult to tell when meals were served.

The three ladies gathered in the dining room, not troubling to change for dinner as no men would be present. "This is pleasant," Maris said, smiling at her family as soon as Mrs. Lindel had said grace. "We've hardly had time for a good coze since Sophie came home."

"I was under the impression we'd done nothing but talk," Sophie said, passing her mother the salt.

"How are all our friends, Mother?"

"Very well. Miss Ondrea and Miss Aurilla are arguing again. Apparently one took the landau out without asking if the other meant to use it. Which one did it, I don't know, and it doesn't matter. If it weren't that bone of contention, there'd be another."

"Don't they ever agree?" Sophie asked, remembering the night she'd arranged the place cards.

"Not in my memory. They sometimes exist in a state of armed truce, but never peace."

"Why didn't either of them marry, do you suppose?" Maris finished her soup. "If they had other people to think about, perhaps they wouldn't be like that."

"Some people are just naturally quarrelsome," Sophie said, wishing to avoid another discussion of marriage. Though neither her mother nor her sister had mentioned Dominic, she knew them well enough to guess what ambitions they had for her. "Others can get along with everyone. And then there is Miss Menthrip, who seems like a dragon but has the heart of a lamb."

This attempt to alter the focus of the conversation might have succeeded except that the servants entered, changed the plates and went out, leaving the ladies to their venison.

"Most men are more quarrelsome than women, I think," Maris said. "Not Kenton, of course. Why, he and Dominic have been friends for years and never a cross word."

"But they are men of especially equable temper," Mrs. Lindel chimed in. "Why, I've never seen Dominic out of temper yet. Even when things go amiss, he always seems to find a reason to be pleased."

"Yes," Sophie said when they both looked at her. "He's everything amiable. A true gentleman. It makes one wonder whether there is something to the theory that blood will tell."

"Oh, yes," Mrs. Lindel agreed. "I think you can always tell a gentleman who was born a gentleman, instead of those trumped-up fellows, 'pickle lords' they call them."

"Mother . . ." Maris said, rolling her eyes. "You know Lord Caventry meant well."

"What's this?"

"Oh, when Mother was in London she made rather a hit with an elderly gentleman. He made his fortune in supplying bullets to the Army."

"Did he make improper advances, Mother?"

"No, of course not." But the girls noticed that their mother's cheeks had grown pink.

"Mother! You never told me."

"They weren't improper. But I couldn't accept any sort of an offer."

"Lady Caventry . . . yes, I could see you in such a role," Sophie said, eager to give out a little of what she'd been taking. "More easily than I could see myself. You would carry the position with a high hand."

"I'd give place to you at table gladly," Maris said.

"You are pleased to tease me, but I assure you it is a position I have no wish to fill. My ambition has always been for you girls, not myself. If I were ever to marry again, I should choose someone of my own station. Reginald Lively, for instance."

Maris and Sophie exchanged startled glances. "Reginald Lively?"

"What's wrong with him, may I inquire? He's a gentleman, I hope. And an attractive one, though I shouldn't say it."

"But he wears a wig, Mother. And a corset."

"What matters that? I like a man to be point-device. He was a good friend to your father and to me. No one has a nicer taste than Mr. Lively. You were saying that you like a man with an equable temper. The only thing that puts him out of temper is an ill-laid table. With his excellent staff, it is a thing that rarely happens."

"Well, he is rich," Maris said.

"I hope I'm not mercenary."

In the silence that fell as the two daughters digested these facts about their mother, Tremlow appeared, but not to continue service. "His grace, the Duke of Saltaire, has just arrived, my lady. He asks if he might join you without changing his attire."

"Goodness me, yes, Tremlow. Show him in immediately," Maris said, putting down her napkin.

Dominic came in with his quick stride. He bowed over Maris's hand, shook hands with Mrs. Lindel, then turned to Sophie, his eyes dancing with happiness. He seized both her hands in his. "You'll never, never guess," he said.

She returned the pressure of his fingers almost unconsciously. "What is it? You're shaking with excitement."

"Can you blame me for it? It's also partly being tired.

I rode half the day." He released her hands when Tremlow touched his shoulder to indicate the place they'd laid for him. It was next to Sophie.

She found herself looking admiringly at the set of his coat across his broad shoulders, splashed with mud though it might be. His boots, too, had quite lost the gloss that was the joy of Fissing's heart, and horsehairs were liberally sprinkled over his breeches. Sophie thought she'd never seen a man so vitally alive and felt a leap of the heart that had nothing to do with whatever he might choose to say.

"Look at this," he said, reaching into his pocket. He brought out a piece of paper, much folded and creased. While he hurriedly ate his soup, in order to catch up with the ladies, Sophie shook open the page.

"It's just the titles," she said.

Her mother and sister were craning their necks. Sophie passed the buff-colored page to them and they read it, heads together.

"Yes, but in order now."

"In order?"

"Look." As she reached to take back the page, he laughed. "Philip gave me three kinds of . . . trouble because I hadn't spotted it myself. I felt no end of a fool when he pointed it out to me."

"I still don't see . . ."

"He thinks it's a map in words. And he thinks he knows what it leads to. I told you—or did I? Anyway, he's the sort of a fellow who has traveled to all sorts of out-of-the-way places and picks up all sorts of queer stories. Then he writes them down and sells the books. Well, he used to. Now he's writing fiction."

Sophie met his eyes and shook her head, still at a loss.

He took the page from her fingers. "Each title has a

certain number of words. See, 'Bronte,' 'Friar Hadrian,' 'Walk Sunset Down.' One, two, three."

"Oh, yes. 'Where White Lillies Grow' is four. 'Heavenward Eyes Reveal Unseen Wonders' is five. Yes." She looked at him with a surmise growing in her mind.

"But they're still meaningless," Maris said. "What does 'Heart of Darkness, Heart of Stone' mean?"

"Though 'Gold of Kings, Gold of God, Hosanna' does sound promising," Mrs. Lindel commented.

"You're quite right, ma'am." Dominic looked at Sophie. "Philip says he thinks these are directions. If you go to Bronte in Sicily and follow these steps, allowing for the poetic point of view, you'll find something. Something Broderick found."

"Bronte is near where he died," Sophie said. "I remember Mr. Knox saying something about it. They'd been staying in the wilds of Sicily for a few weeks, tramping about from town to town."

"What could it be?" Maris asked.

"Well, as I said, Philip is a collector of strange tales. He says that there is a story in those hills about a murdered priest and a missing church treasure during one of the many sackings of that island. There's a thousand such stories anywhere you go in the world, of course."

"Gold of God," Mrs. Lindel said.

"Gold of Kings," Maris said, half to herself. "I wish Kenton were here. He'd find this thrilling."

"Shh," Mrs. Lindel warned, raising a finger to indicate the servants entering.

CHAPTER FOURTEEN

Dominic's news had sent the mystery of the missing manuscript right out of her head. When she did think of it again, the others were deep in a discussion of what they should do with Philip LaCorte's surmises.

"The only thing to do is go to Sicily and look," Maris said. "Find where this 'Friar Hadrian' is and walk off toward the west."

"I agree," Dominic said, "though it's rather long odds that anything will still be there. Someone else may have discovered it by now."

"Why would Broderick go to so much trouble to conceal his discovery in this way unless he was afraid someone would find it?"

"Truthfully," Sophie said, "he would have done it for his own amusement. He enjoyed games, anagrams, puzzles. I should have remembered."

"What do you want to do?" Dominic asked, his eyes warming when he looked at her.

"I think we should follow your friend's advice and write to the consulate in Rome. We need to understand the Italian laws regarding the finding of such things. However, they should know that we only have suspicions, not proof."

"I'll write at once," Dominic said, half rising from his chair.

"After dinner is soon enough," she reminded him gently.

"I suppose. Unless you want to be the one to write?"

"No, thank you," Sophie said hastily. "I've written enough letters for a while. Which reminds me . . . Maris, I left a parcel on the hall table but Miss Menthrip says it never reached Mr. Harley's shop."

"How would she know that?" Dominic asked.

The lifelong residents of Finchley only smiled at him. "She does."

"I shall ask Tremlow what he knows about it. Don't worry. I'm sure there is a simple answer," Maris said.

Dinner passed in a whirlwind of speculation as to what Broderick had found and where it might be hidden. Sophie suggested that it must be up high, or else why look heavenward? Maris put forth the idea that it must be in the dark, which lead Dominic to the conclusion that there would be a cave. "Are there caves in Sicily?"

After dinner, they went in search of books to describe the countryside of that much-contested island. Maris shook her head. "It's time this library had some new books. What use is a library without so much as an atlas? My son will grow up entirely ignorant of geography."

"Here's something," Dominic said, bringing down a large and dusty folio from a high shelf. The spine crackled when he opened it. On the frontispiece was inscribed in two inch letters, *Histoire de L'Abbaye Royale de Saint-Denys en France*. The meticulous sketches, though black on white, gave form to the dreams of avarice. It took no imagination to invest these drawings with the glitter of precious metals and jewels. Busts of saints encrusted with cabochon or crudely cut gems, damasked in gold, sat in quiet dignity next to crosses of every description, from the simple Latin cross, though glorified by gold and gems, to the elaborate fleury cross, which is four crosses joined together at the feet. The one pictured in the book was created by a master artisan out of the most delicate gold wirework, twisted and turned into twining vines. The very picture seemed to live. They could only imagine what the actual object must be like.

"That would certainly qualify as Gold of God," Sophie said, brushing her fingers over the picture of a casket which allegedly held one of the arm bones of St. Peter. It was in the form of a cathedral, the rose window over the miniature front doors created entirely out of jewels. "One could only make so magnificent an object for religious purposes. Anything else would be a defilement of art."

"I don't know about that," Maris said. She turned the book on the desk toward herself, it being too large to hold comfortably. "Look at some of these pictures. The Crown of Louis XIII, the crown of Anne of Austria, the crown of Jeanne D'Evreux, whoever she was, decorated with rubies, sapphires, and pearls. This diadem here is neat without being gaudy. I could see myself in that."

"What year was this book written?" Dominic wondered, turning to the front again. "Seventeen-aught-six." He shook his head, his ready smile fading. "Most of these things are gone."

"Gone?" Maris said wonderingly. "Gone where?"

"God knows. Gold and jewels are portable banks and when a nation suffers a revolution, such things vanish and do not always reappear—and rarely in the hands of their original owners. Most of the gold will have been melted down, many other things broken for the sheer joy of destruction."

"Oh, dear." Mrs. Lindel looked distressed. "So much beauty wantonly destroyed. It makes me feel quite sick."

"Not all, ma'am. Some of the rarer objects were removed to the Louvre, where they still are, unless Napoleon did something with them. But I doubt he did them any harm. He was something of a connoisseur when it came to rarities, especially those of conquered nations."

"You relieve my mind. One day, I should like to go to France," Mrs. Lindel said. She stood up, dusting her fingers. "I had better go to bed. If I am to dance tomorrow night, I must have extra sleep tonight, or I shall never be able to do it. Mr. Lively's parties never break up early."

"I think I'll come up too, Mother," Maris said, yawning in a way that wouldn't have fooled her own infant. "I can't think when I've been so tired."

"I suppose you are right. It's been a long time since I danced. I should keep up my strength." Sophie started toward the doorway but, as she half expected, her mother stopped her with a word and a gesture.

"You should stay and help Dominic write his letter. He *was* your husband, you know."

"I remember. If Dominic . . ."

"I could use your help. Please stay."

While they left, Dominic put the large book back on the shelf, a reach even for him. "I always believed your mother to be a subtle woman."

"Not today. Give them a few moments to retire, then I'll go up, too."

He sat down in an armchair, his legs crossed at the ankles. "What have you been doing while I've been away?"

"Friends and fittings, mostly. This is most surprising

news you've brought back with you. How certain is your friend that his interpretation is the correct one?"

"Philip isn't the sort to admit lack of certainty. He did say that if he turns out to be wrong, he'll buy me a good dinner in Town, but that won't be any good for you."

"What would be good for me?" Sophie went over to the fire, though it meant stepping within touching distance of him. She could have easily trailed her fingertips over the back of his hand with hardly any effort.

"If there isn't anything waiting for us in Sicily . . ."

"I'm not expecting anything. I told you, I think, that Broderick liked playing games. Sometimes they were games without a purpose. I can just see him going to all the trouble of creating a set of secret instructions in order to lead people toward a broken jug that once held beer and a wobbling sign on a spring that jumps out with *Sic Transit Gloria Mundi* written on it. He was fond of adolescent jokes like that."

"So you don't believe we should write a letter to the consul asking him to send someone to look?" In order to see her, he had to tilt his head back. The firelight gilded him until he looked like one of those saints' reliquaries, some handsome, laughing saint like . . . she couldn't think of one offhand. Had a saint ever been martyred for laughter?

"I'm not certain," Sophie said. "In one case, they take us seriously and send someone. On the other hand, they may assume we are a pair of asylum inmates and ignore the letter."

"Augustine Baird won't ignore it. He's the one who always wound up in trouble at school for reading too long, too late, and always the wrong kind of books. He'd leap at the chance to hunt for a genuine buried treasure."

"He's a friend of yours? At the consulate?"

"And one who cannot resist an adventure. This is just

his meat. We'll address it to the consul but send it in a cover to Augustine."

"I wish . . ."

"What?" He reached out casually and took her hand. "What do you wish?"

"I wish I could go myself. Imagine entering a tunnel and seeing the long-hidden gold glittering in your torch-light. The jewels winking red or blue or green fire. The shadows moving . . ."

"The dust. The cobwebs. The bats."

She snatched her hand from his and feigned hitting him. Dominic rose from his chair, all long and lean, a sense of purpose radiating from him. He put one hand on the mantelpiece behind her, leaning in, looking with deep attention into her eyes. She couldn't retreat because of the fire behind her and knew, deep within herself, she wouldn't have retreated if she had a hundred miles of space in which to run.

Sophie started to reach up for his face, wanting to touch the smooth, taut skin over his cheekbones, when the front door slammed with a report like a cannon and Kenton called out a greeting. Nearly as loud was Dominic's clearly enunciated, "Damnation!"

Dominic awoke and threw off the coverlet, reveling in the best of good moods. True, he suffered a little from frustration, but he had high hopes that ere long his hopes would be satisfied. The look in Sophie's eyes last night had been unmistakable. She would have kissed him if Kenton hadn't chosen that moment of all moments to come clattering in. Though Kenton was his best friend, Dominic could have wished him to the devil in that instant.

But here was another day, the sun melting the snow,

in which kisses might be had. There was to be a dance as well, with attendant possibilities for romance. Dominic only wished that Fissing were here to turn him out to his best appearance. Tremlow was an excellent valet in a pinch, but he did not have the dedication to one ideal that Fissing possessed.

Knotting his cravat carelessly, though he had painstakingly shaved, Dominic left his room to eat breakfast. Kenton sat there, turning over the pages of a large book that Dominic thought he recognized.

"Maris bring you up to the moment on what we discovered?" he asked, taking coffee.

"She did. It sounds like something out of a fairy tale. I find it hard to believe that Broderick Banner, of all men, found Aladdin's Cave."

"Strange things happen to poets. His death, for instance."

Kenton closed the old book upon memories of kings and churchmen. "I wondered about that myself. It seems very coincidental that a man should die immediately following such a discovery."

"We don't know it was immediate."

"Let us say within a very brief span. Does Sophie know when her husband went to Sicily and when he was to return?"

"She said he died a few weeks after he went there. And look here, old man, I'd appreciate it if you'd refer to Broderick Banner as her *first* husband."

A slow grin spread over the other man's countenance. "Sits the wind in that quarter?"

"It does." Dominic buttered toast with a confident air.

"Does she know it?"

"I think she has a fair grasp of the situation. I've asked her twice now."

"She's turned you down, I take it." Kenton leaned forward, both elbows on the table. "Well, they're a strange family. So natural, levelheaded, even nonchalant about the little irritations of life. I've seen them take in stride things that would send any other woman shrieking about the room. It's an excellent quality in a wife. And yet . . ."

"At bedrock, they're sheer stubbornness."

"No," Kenton said thoughtfully. "Not stubborn. It's just on some points they feel it's wrong to yield. They'd never compromise a deeply held principle, not even for the men they love. If she loved you, she'd fight for you like twenty tigers, but if you acted in a way that she found unprincipled, she'd turn away. She'd still love you, but she'd turn away and you'd never get her back."

"A pity Broderick Banner didn't understand that. Even so, she stays loyal to his memory."

"Loyal to his poetry, yes, but not to him. She didn't love him anymore. He had no excuse, you know. I told him the same thing I've just told you. The difference is . . . I don't know if he didn't believe me or he just didn't understand. He stood there, his chin raised above a ridiculously high cravat, and told me that a woman had not the wit to hold moral precepts; they were able only to follow the mouthings of propriety. I could have struck him for it, but I didn't want to embarrass Sophie by marrying her to a groom with a black eye. Now I wish I'd put him to sleep."

"A pity these modern houses don't run to oubliettes and lye pits," Dominic said, slicing viciously into some ham. "I don't care if he found the Ark of the Covenant, I'd blot him out before I'd let him marry her, if I knew then what I know now."

"It's unchristian to say it, but I can't regret not having to introduce him as my brother-in-law. Not to mention I've probably saved thousands of pounds. If he wasn't the sort to run into debt and apply to family to be extricated, then I'm a Dutchman." He opened the book again.

"It's a good thing we both have alibis, isn't it?" Dominic said with grin. "Have you ever been to Sicily?"

"No. Have you?"

"No. But I'm going."

"Are you indeed? Following your letter to the consulate?"

"I'm not writing. I'm carrying the message in person. I'll take Sophie with me, if she'll have me. I want her to see his grave and know that the son of a—"

"Here you are," Mrs. Lindel said. "Maris not up yet?" The two men stood up as she came in. "Never mind, never mind. Go on with your breakfast."

"Maris had a busy night," Kenton said. "The baby seems to be hungry all the time."

"That's as it should be. He'll grow up fine and strong. I'm glad to see Sophie is sleeping in as well. I didn't like the way her color kept coming and going all evening. I do hope she doesn't have a fever."

Kenton cleared his throat and shot an amused glance at Dominic. "What do you care to do today, old man?" he asked. "Not riding, I fancy."

"No. I'll go for a walk. I have some matters to think over."

His dreams of a wonderful future kept him company as he walked in the woods. Despite it being not far off the shortest day, the temperature had risen several degrees. Everywhere came the drip of water off leaves and the trickle of small courses running under the snow and down hills. Dominic took off his coat and walked with it over his arm. The trees looked clean and expectant, buds waiting for the spring, of which this day was a foreshadowing. Snow would come again in January, but the trees waited in hope.

Walking back to the house, Dominic saw that Sophie's window curtains were still closed. He entered the library from the rear of the house. Maris had come downstairs. Though neat in her dress as always, her pretty eyes were puffy and her lids seemed almost too heavy for her to hold them open. She sat with her mother, leaning her head on her hand, hardly able to conceal her yawns.

"Honestly, Maris, you should go back to bed," Mrs. Lindel said, taking another stitch in the sampler she was embroidering.

"I was too hungry to sleep anymore."

"That's all well and good. You've eaten now. Go back to sleep. *Sophie's* still sleeping."

"She is?" Dominic glanced at the clock. The hands stood straight up. "That's unusual, isn't it?"

"I think her journey and all the excitement we've had recently have finally caught up with her. You can only go for so long on sheer force of will. She'll feel all the better for a long sleep." Mrs. Lindel also glanced at the clock. "I shall take her a tray at two. That will give her sufficient time to eat and dress for this evening. Such a pretty dress," she said with seeming inconsequence, nodding at Maris.

"Miss Bowles has outdone herself," she answered between yawns. "Oh, dear. I think you are right, Mother. I had better lie down for a little. I'm so glad I'm not going with you tonight. Kenton would have to hide me among the potted palms like Sleeping Beauty in her wood."

Dominic sat down to write a letter, not to Augustine Baird in Rome but to Philip, explaining the family's reaction to his theory and outlining his own plan to travel to Italy after Christmas to investigate the matter personally. After that, since there was more than an hour to wait for Sophie's appearance, he sat down in the armchair, put his feet on the fire's fender and went to sleep.

He was awakened by a frenzied shaking. Mrs. Lindel bent over him, shaken out of her habitual calm. "I can't find Sophie. She's not in her room, and those maids are gone, too."

"Did they go for a walk?"

"No, why would they?"

"Did you ask Tremlow?"

"He doesn't know anything. He muttered something about a ham and a parcel and half holidays, then hurried away. Very unlike him."

When they were all gathered together, Dominic addressed the household, with Kenton's permission. "There are only two choices. One, that Mrs. Banner left this house of her own accord and without a word to anyone. Two, that she left under some sort of compulsion."

Maris clung to her husband's arm. "What are you saying?" she asked. "Do you believe she's been abducted? By her maids? They didn't seem to be that sort of girls."

Parker, the upstairs maid, raised her hand hesitantly, egged on by some of her cronies. "Begging your pardon, Your Grace . . . " She faltered, looking about her for support.

"If you have anything of substance to add, Parker, pray do so," Tremlow said in his old majestic way, though his face looked drawn and pale.

"I'm in the room next to those girls, and one night, about two days after they'd come, I thought I heard a man's voice in their room."

"Why didn't you say something about this, Parker?"

"I did, Mr. Tremlow. I asked the one that spoke better English about it, just teasing like. She looked awful fierce and, having been dusting the desk which I was showing her how to do despite it not being my proper duty . . ."

"Go on, my dear," Dominic said, forestalling Tremlow's incipient outburst.

"She picked up the paper knife and stabbed the blotter, Your Grace. I was that frightened, she didn't look hardly human."

"That's what she told me," piped up the nursery maid.

"Why didn't you tell Mr. Tremlow or Mrs. Lemon?" Maris asked.

For the first time, Parker looked abashed. "The other one, Lucia, gave me some ribbons and begged me not to say anything. And Mrs. Banner . . . well, she'd asked me to be kind to 'em."

"Thank you, Parker," Dominic said. "If anyone has anything else to add? No?" He looked at Kenton, who started to dismiss them, when Mrs. Lindel spoke.

"Simms, the day after the baby was born, you said something to me about strange men in the halls."

"Did I? Oh, yes, I did," Simms said, cradling the heir of the house in her arms. "I saw a man, someone I didn't know, in the upper hall a few days after Mrs. Banner arrived."

"What did he look like?" Dominic demanded.

"Ever so strange, Your Grace. I said to myself, 'You look ever so strange.'"

Mrs. Lindel spoke in a whisper to Dominic. "She's making that up, now that she thinks there's something wrong. She probably didn't think he looked unusual at all. She just didn't recognize him."

"Thank you, Simms," Dominic said. He glanced at Kenton, who dismissed the servants.

Tremlow stayed behind. He expanded upon the disappearances from the house, the ham, the manuscript, and the irritating way in which the Ferrara girls came and went at their own sweet will, now aggravated by this new mystification. "I don't like mysteries," Tremlow said firmly, quite forgetting honorifics. "They make for an unsettled household and I have always striven for calmness, serenity, and order. I will search out those responsible and I trust they will be instantly discharged. Your Grace, my lord, my lady, Mrs. Lindel, pray accept my apologies for these occurrences."

"Not your fault, Tremlow," Dominic said and the others echoed his sentiment.

"On the contrary, Your Grace, a butler is like the captain of a ship. Anything that happens is ultimately his responsibility. We butlers accept this unquestioningly. I will wipe out this blot upon my honor." He bowed and departed.

"I never realized Tremlow was such a *preux chavalier,*" Mrs. Lindel said in admiration.

Dominic paced up and down, his hands tucked behind his back. Somewhere in his mind, a tiny voice was screaming out panic and alarm. He couldn't silence it entirely, but he could refuse to listen. "She's somewhere," he said. "Somewhere nearby. Mrs. Lindel, go to Finchley. Ask everyone if there were any carriages passing through last night. It's the only road they could have taken, correct?"

"Yes, they would have had to pass through town in anything heavier than a drag," Kenton answered.

"I don't need to ask everyone," Mrs. Lindel said. "Just Miss Menthrip. I'll tell her the whole tale. She may be able to suggest something."

"I'll come with you," Maris said. "I care not a jot for the conventions."

"No," Mrs. Lindel said in that motherly tone that admits no argument. "Your baby needs you. I can handle Miss Menthrip."

"We'll await events," Dominic said. "Then the guilty had better watch out."

CHAPTER FIFTEEN

Sophie wanted to wake up. She wandered lost in a dream in which she walked among people she knew well, speaking to them, dealing with them in an ordinary way, yet fully aware all the time that each face was only a mask hiding some horror. Darkness seemed to follow her. Yet when she turned to confront it, there would be nothing there. She struggled as if in deep water, striving helplessly to rise through her dream to waking day.

She lay facedown with her head upon a pillow, her hair hanging over her face like a mat of ivy upon a wall. She lifted her head, reaching to paddle her hair away, but could not move her arms. She tried again and felt rope scratch her wrists. Her feet, too, were bound.

She fought to roll over and sit up on the bed. The quilt she lay on was pieced together from blue toile and flowered dimity, old bedroom curtains and dresses her mother had worn as a girl. She knew it well. It had covered her bed at Finchley Old Place for as long as she could remember. What was it doing here?

Rolling over made lights explode behind her eyes. She groaned without realizing it as she sat up slowly. Her hair was driving her mad, in her mouth and eyes, but to flip it aside meant bringing on the pain again. Nevertheless, she tossed her head, her hair flying back to lie in place again.

When she came to a second time, she lay on her back, looking at a ceiling she'd seen more mornings than she could count. The bulge in the far corner of the ceiling was as well known to her as her own nose. What was she doing at Finchley Old Place and in such a condition?

Her hair was out of her face, thank heaven, but her hands and arms were all pins and needles. More cautiously this time, Sophie sat up. The pain in her head seemed more localized, radiating out from a spot behind her right ear.

Sophie tried to draw her memory down to the present and failed. She remembered coming within a moment of kissing Dominic, the expression in his eyes as he leaned down, and then the sharp pang of disappointment as Kenton entered. She'd excused herself and retired to her room. She could remember with great vividness her hand resting on the doorknob as she paused, wondering if it would be terribly obvious for her to return downstairs, ostensibly searching for a book. Wouldn't it be plain that she was hoping to be alone with Dominic again?

After that, everything else was blank.

Longcloth curtains hung over the east-facing windows, glowing with yellow light. Sophie struggled up and rested her sore head against the cool iron post of the bedstead. It was morning, by the looks of things, and she'd retired not much later than half-past ten on the previous night. At least, she hoped it was the previous night. At a minimum, she'd been missing from Finchley Place for eight hours.

Her mouth was parched. The tingling in her hands increased as circulation was restored. She flexed her fingers to encourage it as she gave her mind a problem to solve. Never mind who had abducted her. The question of escape came before all. One element was in her

favor. She knew this house. She knew which stair riser
creaked, which doors led to the exterior and which to
rooms with no other exits, which windows slid up
noiselessly and which shrilled like the souls of the dead.

Sophie drew her feet close to her thighs and tried to
work her arms from behind her. If she couldn't manage
to slip the rope off, then she'd gnaw it, if that's what it
took to be free. Before she'd half begun to wiggle, she
heard footsteps beyond the door and muffled voices
speaking fast.

Sophie froze, unsure of whether to feign sleep, but
the footsteps and the voices moved off. Perhaps she
should have shouted. Perhaps they were looking for her.
Then she wondered why she was not gagged. If she
shouted, who would hear her? Who, for that matter, had
brought her here?

Whoever it was hadn't proved much of a hand at
knots. The rope separated before she'd brought her
hands under her feet. Sophie sat up, rubbing chafed
wrists, and began working on the rope that held her feet.
Though she broke nails picking at the knot, it took only
a few minutes before she was upright and striding
across the floor as quietly as possible to fully restore her
cramped limbs.

With a lift of the heart, she found her shoes on the
floor, just as if she'd slipped them off before getting into
bed. Holding them in her hand, she listened carefully
at the door. She heard nothing. To redouble precaution,
she bent and peeped through the keyhole before ven-
turing to open the door slowly and with great care.

She stepped out into the hall, keeping to the center of
the boards. Three doors to pass and she would be at the
head of the steps. A moment to hurry down them, avoid-
ing the fifth step which groaned rather than creaked,

and out the door. She might not even stop to put on her shoes until she reached the woods.

"I'm glad you're awake, Sophie," a man said from behind her.

She jumped, startled, but did not utter a sound. Turning, she saw Clarence Knox sitting on a straight-backed chair just out of sight of the open door. He'd rocked the chair back on its rear legs to rest against the wall while he pared his nails with a wicked-looking clasp knife. He wore a buff waistcoat, a none-too-clean white shirt, and riding breeches with a piece missing from the knee. A black leather satchel lay on the floor, two or three familiar papers disgorging from it.

"I thought I saw you yesterday," she replied, not wishing to give him any further evidence of consternation. Impossible to imagine being afraid of Clarence Knox— short, not in condition, and with those pale blue, almost childlike, eyes.

"Did you? And you didn't say hello?"

"You disappeared so quickly, I wasn't even certain I'd seen you go into the Royal Oak."

"Ah, yes. The Ferraras are very good sort of girls but they simply refused to bring me anything drinkable. It seems it's acceptable to steal food, but not wine. Well, when bitten by such a thirst, what risks will not a man take?" He lowered the front legs of the chair. "Whom did you tell about seeing me?"

"No one."

"No one?" He stood up, keeping the knife open in his hand. "Why don't I believe you? You'd best do better than that. I have so many questions, and I don't like it when people lie."

"Questions? Regarding what?" Sophie did not want Clarence Knox to come any closer. Not because she was afraid, but he looked . . . unclean.

"Sicily? Specifically, Bronte in Sicily. Broderick found something there."

"How do you know?"

"How do I know?" he asked with a giggle, pointing the knife toward himself. "I was there. How do you know?" The knife turned toward her, the light playing along the sharp edge.

"I don't know anything."

He came a step nearer. "Lying again, Sophie. No, don't run. Stand very still."

Something in his voice, some giggling menace, told her to obey—for the moment.

"You're so pretty," he said. "When I first saw you, I thought that Broderick was blind not to see how pretty you are. He talked a lot about your soul; he was always talking about souls."

In a small voice, Sophie asked a question. "How did he die? It wasn't an accident, was it?"

"Clever girl. Of course, they all believed it. He'd been so sick. What was a sick man doing tramping through such dangerous places? Easy to believe he'd lost his head and fallen, and if there was one more head wound than was obvious, well, that would be my cleverness against their stupidity."

"So clever," Sophie said evenly, nearly sick at this casual confession. "Yet he found it, not you."

"That wasn't cleverness," Clarence Knox said, saliva spraying. "That was luck. One day when we were out scrambling over those filthy roads, it started to look like rain. Great black clouds blocking the sky. I wanted to go back. I hate thunder. He went on, leaving me to walk back by myself. That's when he found it. He took shelter in a cave and there it was."

"What? What did he find?"

"Treasure." Clarence Knox's eyes glittered as he remembered, glittered like the knife he balanced on his forefinger, a dirty bandage wrapped around the nail. "He showed me one thing, a broken thumb from a saint's hand, as big as a real one. It was pure gold with an opal set in the nail. He said that the rest of the hand was there and that it was the least of all the treasure. I sold it to pay my passage for an eighth of its value. I'll do better next time."

"He showed you where the treasure was?" Sophie felt as if she stood trembling on the point of a compass needle. If it swung, if Clarence Knox's mood changed, she'd fall.

"No, curse him. Curse him. He fell ill from getting soaked through. He said the cave was cold. He fell ill, fever burning him up. He talked, babbling of heaven and miracles and gold. The patron of the inn wanted to turn him out. *I* tended him; *I* sat by his bedside and listened."

"You were his friend," Sophie said softly, but he went on as if he hadn't heard her.

"When he recovered, I asked him questions, but he pretended not to know what I meant. Even when I showed him the thumb, he pretended that he'd forgotten, that the fever had burned it out of his head. I knew he hadn't. When he got better and started to walk around again, I followed him everywhere. One day, he went to a cave. I thought he'd led me to the treasure at last. I imagined what it must look like. All that gold. All those jewels. On the way back, I . . . he fell."

She knew what he meant. "It was the wrong cave," she said.

"Yes, curse him. What business had he leading me to the wrong cave? Him and his wild ideas. He wanted to give the treasure to the people of the island. He didn't want to be like Elgin, raping treasures away from the people. The people? Peasants, living like pigs. What good will any of it do them? It will be mine. I will live like a god."

The knife, carelessly toyed with, became a living thing, charged with malice. Clarence Knox pointed it at her. "You know where they are."

"No. I don't."

"I searched his luggage. I searched the house he shared with that strumpet. I searched your house. Only afterward did I realize that the answer must be in the poems. He wrote no letters after he was ill. It must be in the poems."

"But you have the poems. The ones that didn't make it to the post."

He looked surprised, drawn out of his obsession with the treasure. "You discovered that? Bet you don't know how I got them. Why, my dear little wife brought them to me. You didn't know I married Angelina while still at Rome, did you?"

Sophie shook her head. Would she have time to turn and run down the stairs? Could she open the front door before he could catch her? He seemed terribly comfortable with that knife. Could he throw it? All too paralyzing to picture the blade in her back and her life leaking away with her blood. And she would never see Dominic again, not even for one instant to tell him all that she felt.

The thought of Dominic drove the fear out that held her impotent. Though now certain that the Ferrara girls were somewhere in the house, Sophie didn't know where they were. Would they stop her? Did they know Clarence Knox had been driven mad by greed? Did they care?

Clarence Knox took another step toward her. "I've read the poems, Sophie. Broderick couldn't write a decent line, but he was clever. There must be some secret hidden in the poems. A code. You're going to tell me what it is."

"I don't know . . . wait! There was one thing that struck me as odd."

"Yes? Yes?"

"I can't explain. I shall have to show you. Do you have the poems here?"

He couldn't help himself. He turned his head a fraction to look at the satchel beside his chair.

Instantly, Sophie ran and jumped onto the banister, praying to the gods of fools and children that she'd lost none of her old skill. She felt the wind pulling at her hair as she rode down, unable to restrain a whoop of triumph. As she landed, she stumbled, losing a precious second. She ran to the door, fumbling at the locks.

She'd opened it, pulling it with all her strength when Clarence Knox threw himself against it, slamming it closed when she'd been only inches from freedom. He seized her hair in his fist and banged her head hard on the oaken panel. Dazed from the second blow in less than twelve hours, Sophie felt her bones dissolve as she slid down to the floor.

She did not lose consciousness. She could see through the shadows before her eyes and hear despite the buzzing in her ears, but she couldn't make her body respond to any command. The Ferrara sisters came running in, curious about the noise. Though they spoke Italian, Sophie heard it as if in English.

"What have you done, you madman?" Lucia demanded, throwing herself down beside Sophie.

"Don't talk to him like that," Angelina said. She turned to her husband with a warm smile, touching him caressingly. "Are you all right, my darling?"

"Shut up," he said, throwing off her hand. "She's not hurt," he said, panting like a man who'd run a long way.

"No?" Lucia spread open the fingers of the hand that had been exploring the back of Sophie's head. "What do you call this? Marinara sauce?"

"Oh, the poor lady. We'll take care of her."

"So he can put her to the question? You're as crazy as he is. Don't you think they'll be looking for her?"

"They won't find her before she tells me what I want to know. Wake her up," Clarence ordered.

Angelina looked at her husband with great love shining in her beautiful dark eyes. "You should rest. I'll make gnocchi. You like my gnocchi; it's the best in Rome. You haven't had a bite since last night."

"I don't want anything. Leave me alone." He hardly looked at her, staring constantly at Sophie, watching for any sign of life. Angelina shook her head and went to kneel down beside her sister.

"She doesn't look so good. I don't like her color," Lucia whispered.

Angelina propped Sophie against her shoulder. Sophie moaned when she was moved and the pain seemed to bring her back to her senses. She blinked against the light that seemed so bright.

"Is she awake?" Clarence came closer, standing over them.

"She's coming around. Lucia, get some water."

"Yes, bring the bucket. Some water sloshed over her will wake her up," Clarence said eagerly.

Lucia stood up. "You're both crazy," she said, but went off to do as she was told.

Sophie wanted the man to go away. His presence was like a suffocating cloud of fear. She couldn't think clearly and she associated this more with him than with the two blows on her head. She could feel blood trickling onto her neck. "The poems," she said in a whisper. "The answer is in the poems."

"Do you hear, Angelina? I was right. What about them? What about the poems?"

"Can't tell you. Show you."

"I'll get them." He spun around and sprinted for the stairs, taking them in great leaps.

"Let me help you up," Angelina said in her ear. "Show him what he wants to know. I promise you'll be safe after that."

"He'll kill me."

"No, no. I won't let him. We'll put you back into that nice room and before we leave for Italy, I'll tell someone where you are."

"Here's the water. Where's the crazy man?" In one hand Lucia carried a heavy oaken bucket, banded with blackened steel. In the other, she held a tin tankard. "Oh, she's better."

Sophie still leaned heavily on Angelina. "Help me," she said. She raised her eyes to Lucia. "Help me, please." Her gaze traveled down to the bucket.

Clarence Knox came clattering down the steps, still moving fast, holding the satchel in his right hand, the knife in his left. "I keep dropping the damn things." He looked around and saw a round table against one wall. He dragged it out into the middle of the room, scratching the finish on the wooden floor. He threw back the flap of the satchel and upended it. Pages covered with Sophie's handwriting cascaded out, some falling on the floor.

Clarence Knox threw aside the satchel and bent, gasping, to pick up the fallen sheets.

Lucia dropped the tankard and started to lift the bucket up in order to throw it. Then she shrieked, dropping the bucket. Water flew everywhere. Lucia stood, staring down as if fascinated by her left hand. The handle of a knife protruded there as if it had appeared by magic. She screamed again, piercingly.

"No tricks," Clarence Knox snarled. He strode over to her, his breathing loud in the sudden silence. Without hesitation, he jerked the knife from the wound. Lucia sank to her knees, clasping her wrist as blood welled from between her fingers.

"You. Bring her to the table. Show me the answer, Sophie."

"No!" Angelina left Sophie and ran to her sister. After one glance, she turned on her husband and slapped him before he could come on guard. "You are insane!" Her hands curled into claws and she attacked him, trying to reach his eyes.

He fended her off, seeming to forget about the knife still between two of his fingers. It fell, point downward into the wood. He and Angelina reeled back and forth, slipping in the water, tripping over Lucia.

Sophie, standing but swaying like a sapling in a wind, became aware that someone was pounding on the door. It seemed very far away, but the constant sound began to disturb her with a sense that this was somehow very important. Slowly, still as if her body had to translate every message, she began to work the lock. Either it was very stiff or she was growing weaker.

Even before the door swung open, she knew who she would see.

"Sophie!" He seized her as she began to fall.

"Dominic." She smiled at him as she would have smiled at a dear memory. "I love you. Did I tell you that already?"

"You're hurt."

"Only slightly . . ."

A shattering shriek rang out, louder than Lucia's

when she'd been wounded, comprised of all the misery and loss in the world. "Clarence! Clarence!"

Angelina, on her knees in her clinging wet dress, pulled at the buff waistcoat of her husband. He lay very still, only his head lolling.

"He's dead," Lucia said dully. "He fell on his knife."

"No, no. It's there. Look. There's not a mark on his body." She pointed with a shaking hand to where the handle lay, snapped from the blade which lay some inches further along. Yet Clarence Knox lay dead.

"Then the evil spirits came for him," Lucia declared. "You are well out of it. He was bad, that one. A very bad poet."

Sophie awoke in a strangely familiar room. Her hair lay over her shoulder in a neat braid which, oddly enough, ached. The coverlet was drawn to her chin and her arms lay outside it, neatly clad in a white lawn nightdress—as was the rest of her, she assured herself after a peek.

Struggling up, for someone had tucked the sheets in too tight, Sophie reached out for the carafe of water and began to pour herself a glass, but her hand trembled so that she was afraid she'd drown herself.

A lean brown hand reached out and took the carafe. "May I help you with that?"

"Dominic? This is unconventional of you. Alone in my bedroom." She sipped the water, feeling as though she'd never tasted it before.

"That's what your mother said." Dominic reached for the bellpull and gave a vigorous tug. "Until I told her we are engaged. She said it would be quite conventional."

"Engaged?"

"Yes."

"I must have loss of memory from being struck on the head. I don't remember that."

He stood over her, his hands on his hips. "Now listen, my girl, you can't greet your rescuer with 'I love you' and not be engaged. It would be too shocking."

"You're quite right." She held out her arms to him. Dominic sat on the bed and wrapped her up in his embrace. Sophie was a little shy about kissing him, but one touch of his mouth on hers made her forget any other kiss she'd ever known.

All too soon, her mother rapped on the door. "I came to see if you felt well enough to come down to Christmas."

"Christmas? Impossible. It's not for two more days."

Mrs. Lindel smiled indulgently. "You've been asleep two days. Dr. Richards said it was nerve stress and you'd wake up when you wanted to."

"I am hungry."

"Excellent." She turned back and took a tray from some unseen maid. "Eat this soup and then let Dominic carry you downstairs."

The house servants had hung up the garlands, rich with gilt nuts and alive with red berries glowing in the golden light of the hall chandelier. A huge kissing ball hung under it. Dominic kissed her so long that the family came out to see what was keeping them.

"The presents are in here," Maris said. "Come on. I've waited long enough."

She sat beside her sister on the window seat, holding her child in her arms. Sophie dangled a cluster of the gilded nuts in front of her nephew, delighting in his random reaches. "Have you named him yet?"

"Of course. Dominic Kenton. We think you should return the favor in a year or so."

"Have a heart, Maris. I don't even know when I'm marrying him."

"Soon, I think, considering the way he looks at you."

"He always looks at me like that."

"Precisely."

Maris received her handkerchiefs from her mother. A few minutes later, a very similar parcel appeared on Sophie's lap. Unwrapping the silk covering, she found a half dozen handkerchiefs. The carefully embroidered initials in a cluster of strawberry leaves were not SLB, but SLS.

Later, when the baby had begun to cry and parents and fond grandmother had gone to see it bestowed in the nursery, Sophie rested against the strong arm of her future husband.

"What happened to Clarence and the Ferrara sisters?"

"Clarence will be buried, for he was certainly dead. Dr. Richards says his heart simply wasn't strong enough to support him very much longer. He said he might have dropped dead at any moment."

"He was doing a great deal of running and fighting."

"He also carried you from this house to Finchley Old Place. You're not heavy, but that's a long way. I should know. I carried you back again."

She was too comfortable to argue. "I suppose Angelina hit me on the head the first time. She must have been very afraid of him. I think he must have been the one to bruise her face."

"I think so too. I hope you don't mind. I'm giving them enough money to go back to Italy, though I'd rather they didn't accompany us."

"I quite agree. I'll write their parents, explaining that they were unhappy here. I don't suppose, while you are in such a generous mood, Your Grace, that you'd consider paying my back rent?"

"Hmm, I'll think it over."

She reached up and brought his face down to hers. After a long, suspended moment, he pressed her head— gently—against his shoulder. "You talked me into it."

EPILOGUE

The Duchess of Saltaire stood on a dusty road in the middle of nowhere in particular. Above her stood a cliff, not so very high, formed long ago when a volcano, which still smoked, erupted and covered the land with lava. Many centuries after that, but still a long time ago, a man fled from those who would pillage his country. His name would never be known, but he found a cave and filled it with treasures. Years passed, rock slid, sheep came and went, followed by shepherds who, though keen-eyed, never saw the cave. Another rock slide, who can say, un-covered the cave just so that an Englishman could take shelter from the rain.

A tall man appeared on the shelf above her head and waved his arms. "Come up, Sophie. Come up."

"All right. *Prego, Padre,*" she said to the slender priest beside her.

Together they climbed the low cliff, helping each other. Padre Adriano's house had been the starting point for Broderick's gothic map of words. By walking west toward the only field outside of Bronte where white lilies bloomed in the spring—though it was summer now—one could look up and see the top opening of a cave. To a ca-sual eye, it looked like black rock.

The two reached the shelf. Dominic was there to help them over the last few feet, the rocks slipping beneath them. "I can't think how he climbed up in a rainstorm," he said.

"God helped him, my son, evidently," said the priest. "Is it there?"

"Yes, Father. It's all there."

They went into the dark opening of stone, vaguely heart-shaped in form. At the end of a tunnel, after a sharp turn, they saw the torches of the workers. Every flame was answered by a blaze of gold. Bright sparks in every color broke the light. Sophie saw eyes in the faces of saints, inlaid with stones. Beside her, the priest dropped to his knees.

Sophie and Dominic clasped hands while the Sicilians prayed.

As they followed the wagonload up the dusty track, Father Adriano asked the question he'd been asking regularly since they'd come to Bronte. "You don't want any of it? It is all for the people of Sicily?"

"That's right, Father," she said again. "Broderick wanted it that way."

"You are certain?"

"I have the word of his murderer."

Since she'd explained the story to him, he nodded. He didn't ask again for a whole week.

They stayed until the papal representative left, but before they sailed from Palermo, Sophie went down to the small Acattolica cemetery, reserved for those not of the Catholic religion. There were no crosses here, only the tombstones, carved with names and dates. A new one, very white and clean, stood above the spot where Broderick lay. She stood beside it for a few minutes but could think of nothing to say. Finally, she laid a small book on top of the grave. The cover lifted slightly in the sea breeze. The pages rippled, showing glimpses of the stanzas he'd written, read by the sun.

Sophie left by the gate. Dominic stood there, leaning with his casual grace against the wall. "Everything all right?"

"Wonderful. I'm very happy."

"I'm not," he said glumly.

"No?"

"The only way to return to England is by sea. You know how I was on the journey out."

"Is that all that's troubling you?"

"Isn't seasickness trouble enough?"

She fell into step beside him, wrapping her arm tightly about his waist. "I can suggest something else to worry about if you would like."

"What's that?" he said warily.

"Kenton Dominic."

"Our nephew?"

"No, he's Dominic Kenton."

He walked on another two steps before turning to look at her. She nodded. The local citizens were treated to the sight of two more mad English, embracing crazily in the middle of the street.